THE ABBOT
OF STOCKBRIDGE

THE ABBOT
OF STOCKBRIDGE

a Simon Shard novel

PHILIP McCUTCHAN

Hodder & Stoughton
LONDON SYDNEY AUCKLAND TORONTO

British Library Cataloguing in Publication Data

McCutchan, Philip
  The abbot of Stockbridge.
  I. Title
  823[F]

  ISBN 0-340-51340-3

Published by Hodder and Stoughton,
a division of Hodder and Stoughton Ltd,
Mill Road, Dunton Green, Sevenoaks, Kent TN13 2YA.
Editorial Office: 47 Bedford Square, London WC1B 3DP.

Photoset by E.P.L. BookSet, Norwood, London.

Printed in Great Britain by Biddles Ltd,
Guildford and King's Lynn.

THE ABBOT
OF STOCKBRIDGE

ONE

It had been raining steadily for a matter of weeks; mostly the kind of penetrating rain that North Yorkshire people knew too well. The sort that could get inside the clothing almost within seconds. Very wet, very cold. The ground sogged, the rivers ran fast, the waterfalls – Hardraw Force and the three falls of Aysgarth in Wensleydale – thundered in fury and sent spray high into the air to form a heavy mist in the vicinity. The stone-walled fields were thick, clinging mud; the miserable fellside sheep found what shelter they could in the lee of the wind-breaks and the fell farmers cursed their lot.

It had been a similar story over the other side, at the western end of the B6255, the road that ran from Hawes, beneath the Ribblehead viaduct on the Leeds to Carlisle railway, to Ingleton not far from the village of Clapham. The path that ran steeply from Clapham up to the great pothole of Gaping Ghyll, a climb of some three miles to the extinct waterfall that lay as a difficult barrier to be conquered before the final rocky stretch to Gaping Ghyll itself, was treacherously slippery. During the apparently unending rain, the climbers, walkers and potholers stayed away. There was in any case too much water in the cave system of Ingleborough for safety, and the flood warnings had been out for some weeks past.

But at last the rain went away; the sun shone, the land began the long process of drying out. The walkers returned; a few hardy persons returned to the steep path, past the man-made lake lying to the right of the upward track.

The first two, a man and his wife, rested in a derelict structure to the left of the track, about half way along towards the entry to Ingleborough cave. A crumbling building of stone, crammed against the rock background, earth covering its broken roof, a building whose original purpose was now long forgotten. It formed a shelter against the wind; inside were stone seats, welcome to a middle-aged couple.

But the woman was for some reason uneasy.

"I don't like it," she said. She gave a shiver. "It's . . . eerie. Don't you feel it, John?"

"No," he said, and laughed. The laugh had a dead sound, as though stifled by a hand, the woman thought fancifully.

She said, shivering again, "It's . . . oh, I don't know . . . as if someone was watching." She repeated, "I don't like it, John. Let's move on."

"If it worries you that much," he said. Getting to his feet he took a look around the walls and roof. Then he gave a sudden exclamation, his gaze seeming riveted to a part of the roof that was sending down spurts of earth and a few small pieces of rock. Once again he laughed, but shakily this time. "Watching," he said. "You could be right."

"What is it, John?"

He said, "I could swear it's an eye. Right in – " He broke off as more of the roof came down. "Out!" he said in a high voice. He seized hold of his wife and pushed her outside. They had just cleared the structure when the roof came down behind them, bringing mud and rock and general debris. And something else, as they saw when they looked back.

A body. A body long dead, with a single eye that stared from its socket, as if balefully, from the debris. Not, perhaps, so long dead; there was flesh, though very putrid, and there was that eye. The body was dressed in what the man believed was a monk's habit, brown in colour beneath the mud, and there were the remains of a girdle.

The call had come down to the Foreign Office security section from the boss himself, Hedge, sounding agitated. Detective Chief Superintendent Shard was wanted immediately. "If not sooner," Hedge's secretary added tongue-in-cheek. They all knew Hedge. Shard dropped everything and went up. He found Hedge in a tizzy, which was not unusual.

"What is it, Hedge?"

Hedge's plump body shook a little: Shard's question had been a shade peremptory, he thought, and it was not a policeman's place to be peremptory. However, he let it pass. He said, "The police in Skipton. That's in North Yorkshire, I understand."

"Yes, Hedge."

"A walking couple. They found a body. Not in Skipton. Near a place called Ingleborough. I don't know if you know it – "

"I do, as it happens. What sort of body, Hedge?"

"Apparently a monk."

"Ah. Have any monks been reported missing?"

Hedge shifted angrily. "I really don't know – yet. In any case there aren't any monks in Yorkshire now, just ruined abbeys. Fountains, Jervaulx, Rievaulx, Bolton Abbey . . . " Henry VIII had ironed them all out centuries before. A skeleton could linger, but Hedge had used the word body.

Shard said, "There's always Stonyhurst and Ampleforth, isn't there?"

"Oh, really, Shard, they're *schools*. Those sort of monks don't get murdered and – and then carried right across Yorkshire!"

"If you say so, Hedge. But what's the connection with the FO, for heaven's sake? I'd have thought the Archbishop of York – "

"Oh, kindly don't be flippant, Shard. This – "

"All right, Hedge. The civil police, then?"

"They do in fact wish to handle it themselves. For certain reasons I do *not* wish that."

"How did it come to be reported to us in the first place, Hedge?" Hedge didn't answer straight away; that fact aroused curiosity in Shard's mind. Hedge had said the call had come from the police in Skipton. The fact of contacting the FO didn't tie in with them wanting to handle the business

9

themselves. As always, Hedge was being devious, but why? Shard pressed: would Hedge please explain a little further?

Hedge wriggled in his chair. "I had a call from the Commissioner."

"*Not* Skipton?"

"Not *directly* Skipton, no. I'm sorry, but I'm unable at this moment to be more precise." Hedge was wriggling like a fish on a hook but his mouth had set obstinately and Shard knew from past experience that he wasn't going to be given anything further on the point until Hedge was ready to impart. Hedge went on rather fast. "It's believed the body was put where it was found a matter of some months ago – they aren't being very precise yet – they're still waiting for a full report from forensic. The discovery was made late yesterday afternoon. A body that came down from the roof of a sort of cave that collapsed. I gather there's been a lot of rain in the north for a long time now. I suppose the body would have been loosened." Hedge paused, and wiped at his fat cheeks with a silk handkerchief. When he went on again there was a grudge in his voice as though the information was coming out painfully. "There is something else, Shard. It may be relevant but I really don't know."

"Go on, Hedge."

"There was a – a sort of medallion came down with the body." He went on, after a pause, with obvious reluctance. "It bore two letters, JR. Inside a circle. Round the perimeter of the circle a word, peculiar. Peculiar with an e, not an a." Hedge looked stonily across the opulence of his office. "And kindly refrain from making a silly pun out of that, Shard."

There was a little more: Skipton police, or some of them, were on drinking terms with the products of Theakston's Brewery, one of these products being a strong ale called Old Peculier. This they had reported, somewhat tongue-in-cheek, Hedge thought, and they had offered a suggestion: Theakston's Brewery was in the small town of Masham, half way between Ripon and Leyburn. Shard knew Masham from odd nights spent in the King's Head Hotel. He knew something else: in the absence of any other evidence the body was being taken as that of a monk, and Shard had once been told

10

by a man he'd met in the King's Head, a man who was drinking Old Peculier with much enjoyment, that historically a peculiar (admittedly with an "a") was an ecclesiastical district or church that was not amenable to the ordinary ecclesiastical authority, examples being the chapels royal, St George's Chapel, Windsor, and St Peter's, Westminster. At one time there had been more than three hundred such peculiars in England. Might Jervaulx have been one of them? And the ruins of Jervaulx Abbey were not so far from Masham.

Some sort of connection? Very vague; but anything was worth consideration. Hedge agreed.

"So what do you want me to do, Hedge?" Shard asked.

"Go to Yorkshire, Shard. Find out what you can about that body. Liaise with the local police, but keep a low profile. And keep me informed."

"So that you can inform the Under-Secretary, Hedge?"

He saw at once that he had touched a raw spot. Hedge started and his pastry-like cheeks took on a flush. "At the present time, this has nothing to do with the Under-Secretary. It will be between you and me alone. Do you understand?"

Shard said, "No. But if you're giving me the order – "

"I am, Shard. You will kindly obey it to the best of your ability."

Shard asked one more question. "Have you any ideas as to what the JR stands for, Hedge?"

The answer was immediate. "Of course I haven't, none at all." For some reason Shard found himself disbelieving that acid assurance.

Shard, as it happened, was not particularly busy and any work outstanding could be left to his number two. He rang Beth and said he was going north on what sounded like a wild goose chase. "Or wild Hedge chase," he added. He didn't know when he would be back; he never did. Beth was well used by now to being a policeman's wife. If he looked like being away longer than just overnight he would ring from Yorkshire; and then it would be a pound to a penny mother-

11

in-law would be round. Mrs Micklem, who telephoned her daughter at least once a day, never missed an opportunity.

Shard drove the Volvo out of the parking lot and headed for the M1. The Volvo was new and he liked the feel of it. Shard, always ready to take necessary risks in the course of duty, never took unnecessary ones, and in his view Volvos were the safest car on the road, cocooned as they were in their steel frames.

Late that afternoon he crossed the River Ure outside Ripon and headed through the town for the Leyburn road. The King's Head in Masham would be a convenient and comfortable base, at least until things developed.

If ever they did. A dead monk with a curious medallion adjacent above Ingleborough still had no apparent Foreign Office connection that he could see.

After checking in to the King's Head, Shard drove on the short distance to the ruins of Jervaulx.

In London's Tottenham Court Road a short man with a fag-end drooping from his lower lip pushed open a door at the side of a greengrocer's shop, went in and climbed a steep staircase, uncarpeted, that rose from the end of a long passage that smelled of leaky gas jets and boiling cabbage. At the top of the stairs he banged on a door that had a frosted glass panel. The door was opened after half a minute. It was opened by a woman, youngish but haggard and with blonde hair in need of a stylist. She wore jeans and a tank top, the latter strained to its limit over very large breasts.

"Hooky in?" the man asked.

"Hasn't been in all day. Went out just after breakfast."

"Went where, darling?"

She bridled. "Don't you bloody darling me, shortarse. I don't know where he went, do I? Last thing he ever tells me. What you want with him?"

"Just let me come in," the man said. "This is important." He pushed past the woman; the door was shut behind him. Even so, he spoke in a whisper. "I got word that Brother Beamish has come to light. Some nosey bloody walkers, up Ingleborough. I got to let Hooky know, right?"

Shard put the Volvo into the car park across the Leyburn road from the ruined abbey. The ground was still muddy; chickens and small, neat bantams pecked, surprisingly a couple of peacocks strutted, eyeing the car and himself with interest. There was a police car parked; Shard was perhaps not the only one to whom Jervaulx had occurred, though it was possible the patrol car had other business. Shard crossed the road, climbed over a stile into the grounds of Jervaulx, once a thriving Cistercian abbey, founded, so Shard had read, in 1156. Now a muddy path led through a herd of cows to a derelict gate that banged behind him, pulled shut by a counter-balancing weight attached to a length of wire. Just inside the gate was a kind of shed with a table, and on the table was informative literature and an appeal to the honesty of visitors to place coins in a slot. Shard, who had a feeling for ancient monuments and their preservation, put a pound coin in the slot. It dropped with a small thud, no clink of other coins. Honesty was not quite what honesty had been once.

There was not a lot left of the abbey: there were signs warning of possible falling masonry, which certainly looked a risk to anyone who walked beneath the towers and arches. But the place was well kept, no weeds, though the grass was long. The ruined walls were in many places covered brilliantly in purple aubretia.

Shard had little idea what he was looking for – his plan had really been just to try to get the feel of the place, get the feel of a one-time monk's environment, look at the ruins of refectories and cells and so on and see what if any thoughts that might produce. Such was the ruinous state, however, that he doubted that any thoughts at all would come.

Something else did.

From around a buttress the familiar chequered cap appeared, on the head of a police sergeant.

Shard said, "Good afternoon. Is this – "

"Tourist, are you?" the sergeant interrupted, and gave Shard the feeling that he was about to be requested to move on. "If so – "

"Not a tourist." Shard brought out his FO identification.

"Detective Chief Superintendent Shard, FO security."

"Sorry, sir," the sergeant said. "Would you be looking for Chief Inspector Matthews?"

"From?"

"Come over from Skipton, sir."

"In that case yes, I am." This was a stroke of luck; Shard had intended driving over to Skipton next morning; this chance meeting could save him the journey. He followed the sergeant round the buttress. A tall man in plain clothes was walking about moodily, poking at bits of ruin as though stones might speak and reveal all. This was Chief Inspector Matthews; Shard introduced himself.

"I know the name, Mr Shard. I was told . . . though what the heck this has to do with your bunch I *don't* know. Can you throw any light?"

Shard grinned. "None at all. I'm as much in the dark as you, Chief Inspector."

"But you reacted to the Peculier?"

"Yes. What's the view in Skipton?"

Matthews shrugged. "Very open. Murder, or misadventure could be. Slipped and went down a hole . . . a mini pothole. Scarcely suicide." He laughed grimly. "I could think of better ways. No, murder's the most likely, of course – "

"Wounds, any signs?"

"Not according to forensic, Mr Shard."

"H'm. No identification yet, I suppose?"

"No. All places where monks hang out have been or will be contacted, result nil so far. No-one's missed a monk. You'd think they would, wouldn't you? Close communities and all that. Monks aren't two a penny. Not these days."

Shard nodded. "What brought you here, Chief Inspector? Same as me – get the feel of monasteries? Or was it purely the Peculier?"

"The Peculier," Matthews said. "Masham – you know?"

"Yes, I do. Though at this moment I don't know a damn thing else. Can't even begin to reconstruct a scenario. A monk is murdered and the body buried in ground overhanging a stone base as I understand it, and the grave collapses owing to the heavy rainfall and the body scares the life out of

14

a couple of walkers."

"And the medallion. That must have got missed by the killers. Or even dropped by them."

"Yes, the medallion."

Shard didn't add that he believed the medallion to be the reason Hedge was involving himself, the reason, too, why Hedge had been in such an obvious tizzy that morning. There was, in Shard's view, more surrounding Hedge than had so far met the eye. Looking back, it had been as though Hedge was expecting him, Shard, to protect him in some unspecified way. Or if not quite that, then to act as some kind of buffer.

But why? If Shard was right, the reason why should emerge before long. If there was anything clandestine behind Hedge, Hedge would panic sooner or later. Sooner rather than later; Hedge had never been made of very stern stuff.

Shard walked around with the chief inspector from Skipton. Matthews had the medallion in a Cellophane envelope; he showed it to Shard. It told him nothing beyond the little he knew already. His imagination peopled Jervaulx, the old abbey in its heyday, one of the most important places in the North Riding – along with Middleham Castle just up the road towards Leyburn from which in the days of Warwick the King-Maker the whole of England had been ruled. He saw the assembled, habited monks at prayer in what was now an open, grassy space; he saw them with bowed heads, walking the cloisters in meditation. He saw the tonsured heads . . .

"Was the body tonsured? The head?"

"Yes. What does that prove, Mr Shard?"

"Nothing, I suppose. It occurred to me that the monk effect could be a red herring. A body got up to look like a monk . . . but of course even a fake would have been tonsured for realism. All the same, it just might help if forensic could say whether the tonsuring had been done recently or a long while ago. Even if it had been done after death."

Matthews gave him a sardonic look. "It's a long while since surgeons were barbers, Mr Shard. But I'll put the point. The body's available at forensic if you wish to see it."

15

*　　*　　*

Hedge had left the Foreign Office in mid afternoon; he had
an appointment with his doctor, he told his immediate boss,
the Head of Security. The Head of Security had hoped,
perfunctorily, that it was nothing serious, and Hedge had
hedged, mumbling vaguely about his perennial indigestion
and perhaps an ulcer. His appointment had been in fact with
a public telephone box, which was a great deal more private
than the Foreign Office lines, all of which were tapped
twenty-four hours a day except for the personal security lines
coloured red and even those could not be relied upon absolutely, not with MI5 always on the scent to charge everyone in
sight with treason, even their own people.

Hedge walked across the Horse Guards, into St James's
Park, across the Mall and up along Lower Regent Street
towards Piccadilly Circus. He disappeared into the underground station and hung about until a telephone was free,
which it wasn't for quite a while. This angered him and
made him even more nervous than he had appeared to
Shard. But patience, if it could be called that, was rewarded
in the end. Hedge pounced in just ahead of what looked like
a Chinese student and dialled a number in South Kensington. After a nail-biting three minutes, the call was answered
by a male voice who asked who was calling.

"You-know-who," Hedge said.

"Oh, it's like that, is it, ducky, all cloak-and-dagger today,
are we?"

"Don't fool around," Hedge hissed between his teeth,
aware of a fat woman within a couple of inches of him,
tapping a pudgy hand on the head of a small boy attached to
her. She could be listening . . . Hedge said, his mouth tight
against the telephone, "And don't call me – what you just did.
Now pay attention. I want to see Mr Crushe-Smith. *Urgently.*
Is he available?"

"No. Sorry."

Hedge sweated. "When will he be?"

"Don't know, do I? He's not here. Gone down to Stockbridge."

"Oh dear, oh dear." Hedge's fingers shook. "I suppose you

16

don't know why, do you?"

"No. Not really like. There was a phone call, that's all I know – "

"Who was the call from?"

"Don't know that either, do I, ducky? Oh – sorry. It's no use you going on at me. All I know is, Wally buggered off to Stockbridge like his arse was on fire, said not to expect him back till he rang, all right? Anything else you want to know, is there?"

"No." Hedge rang off and his place was taken by the fat woman. Hedge was shaking with anxiety and also with anger. There was of course only one reason why Wally Crushe-Smith employed as butler (other people would have said handyman) a person who addressed callers as ducky and spoke of his employer as Wally. Hedge was not accustomed to such familiarity from servants whatever might be their relationships with their masters. Hedge was an important man, not so far from the top in the Foreign Office, which itself was many cuts above the ordinary Civil Service. Hedge was only two degrees removed from the Permanent Under-Secretary of State himself, a man who ranked close to God. However, there was currently more at stake than servants who got above themselves. Hedge knew he had to go down to Stockbridge, a few miles west of Winchester on the A272, as fast as possible. There would be more to talk about now than would be wise on the telephone, even a public one.

Shard dined alone in the King's Head, his mind going round in circles, uselessly. He pondered on the notion that the body might be a fake; as Chief Inspector Matthews had said, you'd think someone would have missed a monk long since and the fact would be on the files in Central Registry at Scotland Yard. But that had been checked out. On the other hand, why try to make out a body had been a monk? There didn't seem, on the face of it, any point in that. And again and again the query: what had all this to do with the Foreign Office, with Security – with Hedge?

After dinner Shard went out, largely for a fresh-air walk before turning in but also, from sheer curiosity, to take a look

17

at Theakston's Brewery where the Old Peculier was produced. He skirted the market square outside the hotel,
turned through an archway, passed some cottages, crossed
the road at the end and walked along Red Lane. Theakston's
was opposite some holiday cottages; there were tall trees
holding a large number of rooks' nests; the rooks had not yet
all gone to bed. Shard just missed a bombing attack as he
crossed towards the brewery. The place was deserted; big
gates were closed across a yard. Shard walked on, round a
corner, round the side of the brewery. Ahead was another
entry to the yard; this time no gate. He went in, found a sort
of exhibition centre – history of Theakston's, how beer was
produced and so on. Of course, all closed down for the night.
Shard looked through the windows without much interest.
Nothing there to help at all; if only he knew what he was
looking for. Frustration and a sense of total uselessness set in.

He left the vicinity of the brewery, going along a footpath
leading through a council estate. He emerged opposite a
bungalow set in the grounds of an immense Victorian pile,
turned to the right and came to the main Ripon-Leyburn
road. Making back by a different route for the King's Head,
he turned right again, passing a filling station. The dark was
coming down now. As he approached the hotel he saw a man
standing outside, a man whom he recalled having seen in the
bar earlier, drinking a whisky by himself in a corner, a man
who had given him a number of interested glances but had
made no move to speak to him.

This man now stopped him on the way into the lobby.

"Mr Shard?"

"Yes?"

"MI5. Name's Wilson." The man showed a pass concealed
in the palm of his hand. "I checked with Reception. I hope
you don't mind. I'm in possession of certain knowledge, and I
knew . . . " He changed tack. "I'd appreciate a word with you
if you don't mind."

"Go right ahead."

"I knew the family of a man who was a monk. I thought
you might be interested."

TWO

Hedge's destination was not Stockbridge itself but a big house set in the isolation of well-wooded parkland some four miles to the north. This house, which, like the home of any country squire of old, bore no name on the big gateway, was approached by a long, twisting drive that ended in a gravelled square in front of double doors above a short flight of stone steps. Hedge parked his car, went up the steps and activated an old-fashioned bell-pull. The resulting jangle from below stairs could be heard through the muffle of a green-baize door.

The front door bore an identification: a polished brass plate read, ORDER OF GOD'S ANOINTED. And in smaller lettering, *The Jervaulx Resurrectionists.*

The wrenching of the bell-pull was answered by a youngish, tonsured man wearing a brown habit. "Yes?" this man said.

"I wish to see the, er, Abbot."

"I'm sorry, Reverend Father is at compline."

"Oh. May I wait? The matter is important."

"You can wait, yes. Who shall I say it is?"

Hedge said stiffly, "I am the, er, Abbot's cousin. That's all you need to know."

"Brother," the youngish monk said reprovingly.

Hedge stared. "I beg your pardon?"

"I am addressed as Brother. Brother Peter. Reverend Father is very particular about that. Politeness, see."

"Oh, very well then, Brother. May I come in?"

The door was swung wide open. Hedge went in. Never mind that this was supposed to be a monastery or whatever, there was opulence around. Thick Indian rugs, parquet floors shining with polish. An old, dark oak staircase, and valuable-looking portraits on the walls, Gainsboroughs and Opies. Obviously, religion paid better than the Foreign Office . . . Hedge was admitted to a waiting room opening off to the left of the hall. He sat himself in a deep leather armchair and stared at more portraits, including one of his highly embarrassing cousin – second cousin really, though quite like Hedge in appearance. Always a thorn in the family's flesh, Wally Crushe-Smith had been worse than any mere thorn to Hedge. Hedge knew perfectly well that God's Anointed and the Jervaulx Resurrectionists were nothing but eyewash. Wally Crushe-Smith had always had other axes to grind, of that Hedge was convinced though he had never been able to establish what these axes were. Nothing that would stand the light of day, he was certain. And he had always kept very quiet about his second cousin, never owning up to the relationship when he had applied for a Foreign Office career on coming down from Cambridge, which had been in the days when vetting was nothing like as penetrating as it had since become. These days, you had to be whiter than white which, on account of the so-called Abbot of God's Anointed, Hedge was not. Or wouldn't be, if anything ever came out.

The wait was a long one; compline was evidently a lengthy process, to be completed before the brothers were dismissed to their cells. Cousin Wally must surely find it irksome; as a youth Cousin Wally had got out of churchgoing at every opportunity. He had been very imaginative when it came to excuses.

At long last Brother Peter returned. Reverend Father would see his cousin now. Compline, Brother Peter said, had taken longer than usual; there had been various sins to be forgiven in the course of it. Brother Peter had not attended compline himself because he had not been in a state of grace owing to a contretemps in the kitchen when he had struck out with a soup ladle at Brother Paul who had called him a so-

and-so little pouf. Brother Paul was also in disgrace as a result. Hedge, who could see for himself that Brother Paul's accusation had been wholly justified, would have thought disgraced persons more than any others should attend compline so that they could offer up conciliatory prayer. But reflected that the phoney Wally Crushe-Smith had always been quite capable of making up his own rules as he went along.

"Please don't for one moment imagine," Hedge said pompously, "that I had any *desire* whatsoever to come to this wretched place."

Reverend Father smiled genially and tugged at a gold cross suspended on a gold chain around his neck. Taking up a crystal decanter he recharged his glass with whisky: single malt, Hedge could see from a bottle on top of a drinks cabinet – Glenturret from Scotland's oldest distillery near Crieff in Perthshire. "You always were the most impossible little prig, Eustace," Reverend Father said. "Why *did* you come if you're so scathing?"

"I came for my own protection," Hedge said angrily.

"Really? Can you be more precise?"

"I can be very precise. You know very well that I hold a *most important* post in Her Majesty's Foreign – "

"Cut out the bullshit, my dear fellow, do," Reverend Father said. "It simply doesn't cut any ice with me – "

"But don't you see – my position, my career – "

"Oh, I've always respected that, Eustace. Well, not respected exactly. I've played along with you, kept myself out of your hair – haven't I?"

"Yes," Hedge said between his teeth, "because you know very well that I could make things very awkward indeed for you – "

"And I for you, dear boy," Cousin Wally said, pointing a finger. "I for you. Don't forget that."

"I don't forget it for one moment. That's why I've come to see you. When I heard you'd gone down from South Kensington."

"Yes, I knew you'd telephoned. Oliphant rang to say so – "

"Oh, really, and I wish you'd tell him not to address me as ducky. I don't care for it."

Reverend Father raised his eyebrows above well-fed cheeks. "You don't? I'm so sorry, Eustace. I'll have words with the estimable Oliphant. Now: what exactly have you come here for? I don't recollect that you've come across with that yet."

"No." Hedge took a deep breath. "Well, here it is and you'll see the seriousness. A body's been discovered up in Yorkshire. Up a steep path near a place called Clapham. I happen to have been told . . . and the police are working on a murder theory."

"Ah. Well, yes, that's useful information."

"It wasn't intended to be merely useful information," Hedge snapped. "There's more to it, anyway. There was a medallion with the body, with markings. These markings included the letters JR. Which could be taken to refer to your wretched Jervaulx Resurrectionists. And in my position – "

"Oh, really, dear boy, we've been into your position already and I'm damned if I'm going to go into it again." Reverend Father paused, then said conversationally, "So Brother Beamish really has turned up."

"Beamish, is that the . . . " Hedge ticked over. He gripped the arms of his chair and stared at his cousin. *"What did you say?"*

"I said, so Brother Beamish really has turned up. It's not entirely surprising, I suppose. Time plays funny tricks, though in fact it's not really so long ago. So what's being done about it, dear boy?"

"I . . . I . . . " Words failed Hedge. Was he now confronted by a murderer, a murderer who was his second cousin? Terror rose in Hedge. He did his best to regain his composure. Licking at dry lips he said, "I think you'd better explain, hadn't you?"

"Certainly I will, dear boy. It's really quite simple." Reverend Father added, "As a matter of fact you come with no more than confirmatory news. I've already been informed by a man in London – "

"The phone call – Oliphant said – "

"Yes, the phone call. Brother Beamish – "

"Why Brother Beamish?" Hedge interrupted petulantly. "I thought monks were given saints' names? I don't recall a St Beamish."

"No, dear boy, Brother Beamish had become one of my lay monks. I don't allow the names of saints to be given to my *lay* brothers, and anyway Brother Beamish was no saint, far from it." Reverend Father gave a reminiscent chuckle. "But you wished me to explain. Keep your mouth shut, dear boy, and I'll do so."

He did. Brother Beamish, he said, had been recruited by Oliphant, who whilst on holiday in the north of England had come upon him sleeping rough in York – Brother Beamish had been a Yorkshireman from Northallerton, a Yorkshireman of good family who had fallen upon hard times. In short, he was a tramp. There had been what Reverend Father, with a smirk, had called an affinity between Oliphant and Brother Beamish. "No need to go into details about *that*, dear boy, I take it you're a man of the world. Suffice it to say that closer intimacy revealed a briefcase concealed beneath such garments as Brother Beamish was then wearing. He was at a loss to explain how he had come by it, but the fact remained that it contained thirty thousand pounds in used twenties. No doubt the proceeds of some crime which would explain why its loss was never, to my knowledge, reported to the police . . . "

Reverend Father went on to reveal that Brother Beamish had subsequently, with his cash, been initiated into the Order of God's Anointed. He repeated that Brother Beamish had come far down in the world. He was lost to his family; he had been a drop-out since the age of nineteen when he had been sent down from Oxford and had drifted, initially living in a squat off the Edgware Road and playing an instrument in the London underground, a flute. Later he had descended to begging and then tramping the country in search, not of work, but of pickings.

"Like the briefcase?"

"Yes, dear boy."

"And no longer in touch with his family . . . so when he was murdered – "

"Which may have been the case. I wouldn't know about that, of course. But I take your point in advance. When he died, there would have been no-one to care, no-one to ask questions."

"Except you, Wally. Perhaps others of your monks. And Oliphant. I take it he disappeared from your Order . . . one would have thought you would have made a report about that, would one not?" Hedge felt he had scored a point. The Abbot of Stockbridge (which was what Cousin Wally called himself) looked, Hedge thought, a shade discommoded. But not for long.

Reverend Father gave a sigh and said, "Yes, perhaps one would think that, but life is seldom as simple and straight-forward as all that, dear boy. The fact is that Brother Beamish, with his education – he'd been at a very good public school, you know – and also his somewhat interesting career since then – Brother Beamish had become quite one of us as the saying goes and very knowledgeable as to, shall we say, the affairs of the monastery. Unfortunately he decided to leave us. To revoke his vows, as it were. I think he found the life constricting, preferring the open road. It was his own choice, you see. And of course there was a fracas, which was most unfortunate."

"Fracas?"

"Yes. Brother Beamish had made certain approaches to one of our novices, little more than a boy really. The boy," Reverend Father added, "socked him one right on the kisser and then really set about stitching him up. It was soon after that that Brother Beamish scarpered. After that . . . well, I really don't know what became of him. Now he's dead, and I'm really very sorry. Prayers will be said, of course."

"It's a little late for that," Hedge said grimly.

"Not for his soul, dear boy. It's never too late for that."

Hedge grunted. "I assume you kept the thirty thousand."

"Board and lodging, dear boy, board and lodging. I'm not made of money, you know."

Hedge shook his head in bewilderment and a mounting anxiety. His cheeks wobbled as he spoke. "I find it strange –

24

after what you just said about his knowledge of the, er, monastery – that you should have simply let him go. Let him get away is what it amounts to. With his knowledge in his head."

Reverend Father's expression altered rather suddenly. "Are you imputing, dear boy, that some sort of chicanery takes place here at Stockbridge?"

"Oh no, no, certainly not – "

"Just as well, dear boy." The tone was icy, a different Cousin Wally now. "Just as well."

"Yes. But I do know you, Wally."

"And I know you, Eustace." Reverend Father put the tips of his fingers together parsonically and stared at Hedge over them. "*Cousin* Eustace, I should say. Cousin Eustace the pompous prat, snobbish pillar of the Foreign Office, Cousin Eustace who preens in the shadow of the great, the important, the leaders of our land. Cousin Eustace who keeps his nose oh, so clean." Reverend Father laughed, and there was an edge to his laugh, a keen edge like a knife. "It's all crap, of course, but one wouldn't expect you to see that. I remember you from way back, Cousin Eustace. Cousin Eustace the prim little sneak, Cousin Eustace who was caught looking up Aunt Mary's – "

"Really, that's – "

"Skirt. And said he'd seen a wasp going up there. At Christmas. No wasps. But you managed to escape a beating."

Hedge's cheeks were aflame. "Fancy dredging up the past like that. If you think – "

"Allow me to continue, Cousin Eustace of the Foreign Office. I concede that the episode of Aunt Mary's skirt and the hypothetical wasp would be unlikely to interest your bosses in the Foreign Office. It would not be on account of juvenile curiosity that you would get the push and fall from a great height into oblivion . . . if you should be so unwise as to repeat anything of what has taken place between us this evening. Do you understand me, Cousin Eustace, or do you not?"

"I – "

"Because it would be in your interests to understand me

very well. And I have been forthcoming in answering your questions for one reason and one reason only: you can be, will be, of use to me. Certain reports have been made to you. You will now do all that you can to have this investigation quashed. Brother Beamish, it appears, is dead. Dead he must remain. If anything is resurrected you will suffer, Cousin Eustace. You can be very sure I shall see to that."

Quaking away from the big house that didn't look in the least like a monastery, Hedge was in a state of utter confusion and fear. Cousin Wally he knew to be a dangerous man and a vindictive one; and when his role had so suddenly shifted from Reverend Father, Abbot of God's Anointed, to Cousin Wally the bane of the family, Hedge had been left in no possible doubt that he meant precisely what he said. The steel had come through; and Hedge could almost feel it biting into his skin. He was now under a clear and bounden duty to make a report either to the Commissioner of Metropolitan Police at Scotland Yard or to the Head of Security. Perhaps, in the circumstances, both. That was what he should do the moment he got back into London.

But he wasn't going to. He wasn't going to take the risk. Cousin Wally would manufacture any lies, any kind of story that would fit his wishes. Anything at all might be said. Hedge had visited Stockbridge. Why? In fact – Hedge quaked behind his steering wheel – to bring a warning about a murder. That was incontrovertible. With his personal knowledge of what the JR on that medallion had meant, or might have meant, he should have gone to the Yard (by phone anyway) and not, absolutely not, to Stockbridge. Already in a sense he had incriminated himself, become an accessory after the fact, or perhaps before the fact or facts if other as yet unknown facts should emerge, as they surely would.

It was a very nasty situation. And inside himself Hedge believed that Cousin Wally had been party to the murder of Brother Beamish and the depositing of the body in the earth, the collapsible grave in the wilds of North Yorkshire. Hedge, as he drove on towards London, bearing the heavy burden of his conscience, had recalled something that struck dire fear into his heart: Cousin Wally had leapt to an immediate conclusion that the murdered body was that of Brother Beamish. That could certainly be taken to indicate guilt, could it not? Yes, it could. On the other hand Cousin Wally surely would have a better guard than that upon his tongue; and of course he had already had the tip-off via Oliphant and some unknown man in London.

It was a most terrible dilemma. One that could finish Hedge in his career if ever he should be discovered to be as it were in cahoots with Cousin Wally.

It was now vital to contact Shard. But Shard was not immediately available. Just like Shard, Hedge thought vengefully, still furious at having been called a pompous prat, no thought for others, only for himself. The police were not what they had once been.

Wilson said the monk's name was Beamish. He said that the churchyard would be a good place for a private talk. Shard concurred; with Wilson he walked past what had obviously once been the rectory, through an iron gate into the peace of the churchyard.

They walked slowly around the old gravestones. The man spoke of Beamish, telling Shard a story of Brother Beamish's background that corroborated what the Abbot of Stockbridge had told Hedge way down south. Beamish had been a drop-out and the family had withdrawn from him as much as he from them. Contact had been totally lost; he had been heard of briefly in Australia, where there had been some difficulty with the young son of a station owner for whom Brother Beamish had worked for a time driving a tractor. After that, nothing.

"But you knew he'd been a monk," Shard said. "How come?"

"I learned that much later, Mr Shard. A man who'd seen him in Stockbridge in Hampshire."

"You know he's dead? That his body has been found?"

"Yes."

"How did you know?"

The man hesitated. "It was a sheer coincidence," he said after a few moments. "In my line it's sometimes necessary to ... let's say, disregard the law in its strictest interpretations. You'll understand about taps. Only this morning I got a crossed line. A telephone in the vicinity of the Tottenham Court Road. A woman was speaking to a man she called Hooky. There was talk about the finding of a body. The body was that of a Brother Beamish from a monastery near Stockbridge. Of course, I went on listening ... but there was nothing further."

"Nothing at all?"

The man shook his head. "No. Obviously, a warning was being passed on – "

"Do you know where to?"

"A number in South Kensington. I have the number here." He passed over a scrap of paper torn from a notebook. This showed the number. No name, but that could easily be established. Shard asked curiously, "With this information to hand ... why come up to Yorkshire and find me? Why not the Met?"

"Because I happened to know you were on the case, on behalf of the Foreign Office. And because I have suspicions in other directions. I'll be brief: the set-up near Stockbridge isn't quite what it appears to be on the surface. They call themselves God's Anointed and the Jervaulx Resurrectionists. I – "

"JR," Shard interrupted. "As I'd thought, a Jervaulx connection. Beamish's body was accompanied by a medallion." He described it. "Did you know that?"

"No, I didn't know that. But having been a lay brother at Stockbridge I suppose it fits. The JR."

"Go on with what you were saying," Shard prompted. "Your suspicions about the set-up."

"Yes. Well, the Jervaulx Resurrectionists – or so I believe anyway – deal in bodies right enough. Live ones. I believe they're in the business of illegal immigration, though I have no proof of that." There was a pause, then the man added, "There's something else, something I found out while working on my theories earlier on. I'll save you the trouble of

28

finding out who lives at that South Kensington number. It's the so-called Abbot of Stockbridge, who doesn't act the abbot every day of the week. His name is Walter Crushe-Smith. And here's another reason I came direct to you. His cousin — second cousin to be precise — is your boss."

Shard stared through the gloom of the night. *"Hedge?"*

The man nodded.

THREE

Hedge had slept very badly. It wasn't just his over-riding anxieties: it was his stomach. Painful indigestion and a constant need for bismuth. When he had reached home he had found a note from his housekeeper: Mrs Millington was sorry, but she'd had an urgent call from her sister-in-law, who was ill with an attack of what sounded like food poisoning, could be salmonella, and she'd had to catch a bus. She would telephone in the morning; meanwhile she had left Mr Hedge's supper in the oven. Supper was done to a burned frazzle and Hedge had had to make do with a salad from the fridge. He'd overdone the radishes and the spring onions and thus had suffered.

Pain and discomfort added to his terrible worries about Cousin Wally. Everything would rub off on him if Cousin Wally was charged in connection with a murder. Perhaps he would do better to spike the enemy's guns in advance, go straight to the Head of Security and make a clean breast of it. But then he would himself be accused – justly, of course – of covering up Cousin Wally all those years ago, and that would be regarded as an absolutely heinous sin in any gentleman in Foreign Office employ. Between his sheets Hedge shivered and took more bismuth in a glass of water. Confound Mrs Millington. Tonight of all nights. He dithered, wondering if it would be unwise to ring Shard in his hotel in – where was it? – Masham.

He almost did, but refrained. Too risky. He must simply be patient. In the morning, he would have Shard ordered back post-haste. And yet even here there was a dilemma: how far should he confide in Shard?

Everything was against him and it really wasn't fair at this stage of his life. He was not so very far off retirement, and now even his comfortable, index-linked pension could be at risk. The Foreign Service could be a hard taskmaster and at times vindictive. During the night Hedge's hot-water bottle leaked. He had always taken a hot-water bottle to bed whatever the weather, since it comforted him to clutch it. Leaking, it was far from comfortable. Really, Mrs Millington should have seen to that before rushing away to her relative's aid. Surely he came first. Servants were such a pest, much too independent, not at all what they had been before the war.

When Hedge reached his office suite next morning, still with indigestion and in a very bleak mood, Shard, who had driven through most of the night, after driving west of the Pennines to view the dead monk, had got to the Foreign Office security section ahead of him. As Hedge was informed by his secretary.

"Oh, good. Send him up immediately. Are there any Rennies?"

"Yes, Mr Hedge, I always – "

"Yes. The Rennies first, then. Two."

When Shard came up, there was the aroma of Rennies; he knew Hedge would be fractious. Hedge was.

"Oh, there you are, Shard. I've been wanting you. You're never there when you're wanted."

"Your orders, Hedge."

"Kindly don't argue, Shard, I don't like it. The fact is, I'm worried about this wretched body. Who – "

"Brother Beamish."

Hedge's mouth dropped open and he gave a fish-like stare. "What was that, Shard?"

"Brother Beamish. The identity of the body."

"How do you know that?"

Shard shrugged. "I was contacted in Masham last night. A man from MI5 – "

"MI5?" Hedge showed alarm.

"By name Wilson. Do you know him, Hedge?"

"No, I don't. Why MI5, Shard? Where do they come in?" Hedge was shaking badly. MI5 was the last interference he wanted.

"Wilson," Shard said, "knows, or knew, the family of the corpse. The corpse of Brother Beamish. From a monastery near Stockbridge in Hampshire."

"Really."

"The abbot of which I understand is your cousin, Walter Crushe-Smith."

Hedge stared glassily, the indigestion rising like a lump of concrete from his stomach. "A distant member of the family," he mumbled. "We don't get on, never have. I know absolutely nothing about him whatsoever."

"You knew nothing of the monastery? Nothing of God's Anointed, nothing of the Jervaulx Resurrectionists?"

"No, I didn't."

"You're sure of that, Hedge?"

"Yes." Hedge was committed now; there could be no reporting his visit to Cousin Wally. That was in any case best kept hidden; there was no reason why it should come out, not unless Wally opened his mouth, which Hedge thought – or fervently hoped – was unlikely.

"So when you said that the JR on the medallion meant nothing to you, that was a simple statement of fact?"

Hedge's face darkened. "Really, Shard, it's not your damn business to – to catechise me in my own office – "

"I'm a policeman," Shard said. "I think as a policeman and I act as a policeman. And I'd like an answer to my question if you don't mind, Hedge."

"Oh, very well. The answer is no. I mean yes. Yes, it was a statement of fact that I'd never heard of – of this JR."

Shard nodded non-committally. "Just as well," he said. "Considering the business interests of the Jervaulx Resurrectionists. I had a long talk with Wilson of MI5 last night." He spoke of the illegal immigration racket operated, according to MI5, by the Abbot of Stockbridge. He said, "They're not the ordinary illegal immigrants, Hedge. Not Indians or Pakistanis or whatever that used to come in that way. It's

32

bigger fish – politically undesirable entries to the UK. Men who upon being landed in various south coast ports, marinas and so on, or on lonely stretches of open coastline, are taken to the care of the Jervaulx Resurrectionists. They're taken on the strength as temporary lay brothers and given temporary identities, not saints' names. Brother Smith, Brother Jones, Brother what-have-you. These people, who don't appear in the light of day until they've been moved on, are a mixed bunch . . . not all of them in fact political. They include big-time criminals who've sought sanctuary abroad in countries having no extradition arrangements and who have a temporary need to return to the UK for various reasons either personal or business. The politicals have included a number of Germans anxious to establish a presence in Britain, some of them neo-Nazis still loyal to the memory of Adolf Hitler, men who might be used as *in situ* spies in the event of any future conflict between us and a united Germany. Wilson – "

Hedge broke in, sweat pouring down his face. "If MI5 know all this, Shard, surely – "

"They don't know it. Suspicions are strong but they've never managed to find proof. Walter Crushe-Smith is a clever man, Hedge. He – "

"So it's all the merest supposition."

"Not quite that, Hedge. As I said, MI5 just hasn't got quite enough to go on. Yet."

Hedge's thoughts raced. Not quite enough yet. Not *quite* enough. Obviously, they had quite a lot, and one day they would pounce. After pouncing they would find out quite a lot more, that could be regarded as a certainty. He, Hedge, next in line to the Head of Security in the Foreign Office, innocent though he might be and certainly was except in the matter of failure to disclose a relationship years before – years before Cousin Wally had become a crook – would be for a very high jump. Did he confess to Shard here and now or did he try to ride it out? The dilemma was now worse than ever. And he shrank from the hard look in Shard's eye, shrank like a shrinking violet from telling him that only yesterday he'd had close contact with Cousin Wally. To go to Stockbridge had been a colossal mistake, but it was one that could not now be

33

rectified. Except, of course, by a confession; and that wasn't on, Hedge decided. He couldn't possibly forget Cousin Wally's threat. Cousin Wally would see to it that he was utterly discredited in the FO.

Shard said, "Did you hear what I just said, Hedge?"

Hedge heaved himself out of a fog bank of terror. "I didn't quite catch it, no."

"It's believed that the biggest fish of all is coming through soon."

"Oh. Who?"

Shard said, "A man, a German, who's known only as Klaus The Long Knife. The reference appears to be to events in pre-war Germany, Hitler's Germany. The Night of the Long Knives – remember?"

Hedge said yes, he did remember. The murders; the persecution of Jews, the burning of the Reichstag, all back in the early nineteen-thirties when the Nazis were in the ascendant and the years were rolling on towards the outbreak of war. Shard went on to say that MI5 had not been able to establish the identity of The Long Knife; the man was shrouded in personal mystery. But it was known that he was a firebrand, an *agent provocateur* with a very considerable underground following in Germany; and it was believed he was a killer many times over.

"What's the purpose in infiltrating him?" Hedge asked.

"Go back over what I said earlier: the possible establishment of a Nazi presence in Britain, a kind of fifth column to be used in the event of a war with a re-emergent Germany. It's not impossible, Hedge."

Hedge said pettishly, "I can't see the connection with that body. The man Beamish."

"Beamish was just a sort of catalyst, Hedge, that's all. Of himself, he's probably not important. The discovery of the body . . . it concentrated some minds more closely on Stockbridge."

"MI5 minds?"

"Yes. And when those boys ferret, they ferret."

"But you said they don't know the identity of this – this person from Germany. That's not good ferreting, is it?"

34

"Maybe not. But things closer at hand can be more easily ferreted, Hedge."

Hedge swallowed hard. "What's that supposed to mean, Shard?"

"Just that I think you ought to search your mind a little more thoroughly, Hedge. You'll have to open up on Walter Crushe-Smith. Even if it's only to the extent of giving us a profile, a background of family knowledge, that sort of thing."

"Oh, no doubt I can tell you a little in that way." Aunt Mary's skirt – but that was Hedge himself and not Cousin Wally – the disappearances of small amounts of money from people's bedrooms when Wally had been present at Christmas gatherings, lies told about who had pushed the cat off an upper storey windowsill. "I expect I can help."

"And anything else that occurs to you," Shard said ominously. He knew Hedge very well indeed, and was more convinced than ever that he was holding back on something. Something – but what? He prodded. "MI5 is not going to let this thing go, Hedge. In a short time they'll be in touch with the Head of Security. I've no doubt they'll be asking for our help. Officially. What do you want me to do now?"

"What do you mean, Shard? You'll just obey orders as usual."

"Yes. No matter what I might dig up?"

"Really, I – "

"Because my first loyalty, to use an old-fashioned word, is to security. And you can read into that what you like. I can't be more specific."

Hedge was about to give some sort of answer, he really didn't know what, when his telephone burred. The Head of Security was on the line. Into the telephone Hedge said, "Yes, of course, at once." Putting down the handset Hedge nodded distantly at Shard. "Thank you, Shard, that'll be all." Dismissed like a servant, Shard left the office.

"A hornets' nest of blasted monks," the Head of Security said but said it without humour. "What's all this about a cousin of yours being the abbot – h'm?"

Hedge's heart seemed to thump aloud. "Yes, Head."

"What d'you mean, yes? We know he is – MI5 knows he is. I'm asking for some sort of explanation."

"Of the fact that he's my second cousin, Head?"

"Not quite. Of how you come to have a connection with what Intelligence believes to be a den of thieves. People acting against the interests of the state. Not quite the thing, you know, is it?"

"No, Head. But a *second cousin* – it's not a *very* close relationship."

"No, that's true of course. And I suppose you can't be held responsible for what a second cousin does."

Hedge breathed a shade more easily.

"Nevertheless, you should have made a report that your cousin was the abbot of a monastery. It could be relevant to, er, security. We do like to know these things." The Head of Security gave Hedge a shrewd and penetrating glance. "Do I take it, though, that you were not aware of the fact?"

Hedge, offered the opportunity of telling another handy lie, took it. "That's correct, Head. We had lost touch . . . we never had much if anything in common." He paused, took his courage in both hands, and plunged in the interest of projecting honesty and a manly desire to shoulder blame where blame was due. "I have to admit I, er, failed to reveal any relationship when I made my application to the FO originally. That was of course wrong of me. But – "

"Black sheep?" The Head asked keenly.

"In a sense. Nothing criminal, of course. Not then."

"No, no. Well, it's understandable. We all have the odd skeleton in the cupboard, old boy. And anyway, aside from that, second cousins do tend to be overlooked, don't they?"

"Er – yes. Yes, they do." Hedge was overcome with sheer relief. He was off the hook.

Or was he?

There was the other hook: his so-recent visit to Stockbridge and his conversation with Cousin Wally, a conversation that could certainly be considered subversive. He started quaking again: if the H of S ever found *that* out, he was really done for. It wouldn't be just his position and his pension: prison would be on the cards. Four to a cell, slopping out, sexual attacks by dubious men with AIDS, riots and razor-blades and uncomfortable roofs. Hedge broke out into a cold sweat and dabbed at his forehead with a handkerchief. The Head didn't seem to be aware of Hedge's agitation. He was pre-occupied, staring into space over Hedge's head and tapping a gold ball-point pen against his teeth. Hedge waited for him to say something, anything to break the somewhat fraught silence.

"Could be quite useful."

"I beg your pardon, Head?"

"The relationship. Walter Crushe-Smith. Don't you see?"

"Er . . . "

"It could be immensely useful. *You* could be immensely useful, Hedge. If you were infiltrated . . . "

"As a monk?" Hedge asked, his mind in a whirl.

"Not as a monk, no. Crushe-Smith would obviously recog-nise you – wouldn't he? Be sure to, what? Even if you've not met for years. No, I didn't mean that sort of physical infiltra-tion. I meant, re-establish the relationship. Long lost cousins, all that sort of thing, long time no see, much to talk about. Get him to open up. Without, of course, revealing your position in the FO. Think you could manage that, do you, old boy?"

"Er – "

"Of course, it's nasty. I don't deny that. Spying – in a sense – on one's own relative."

"Yes," Hedge said eagerly. "There is that."

"Not gentle.nanly."

"No, not gentlemanly, Head."

"But in the wider interests of the security of the realm, don't you see. It would be an immense help to – to obtain inside information. It's absolutely vital we get our hands on this man, The Long Knife." The Head of Security leaned forward and gave Hedge another penetrating look, shrewd, direct, honest, forthcoming, eyes wide. "It would be a feather in your cap, Hedge. An *ostrich* feather, no less." Like a field marshal, but it would never happen, Hedge thought in real anguish. As an object of spying, Wally Crushe-Smith was the

37

deadest of dead ducks. "As a matter of fact, I'll reveal something I perhaps shouldn't: the PM is personally very worried about this incoming German. The facts – I don't know – I fancy they crystallise all her fears about Europe and the loss of our sovereignty, the undermining of the Queen's position, all that sort of thing. And, of course, the whole business of a united Germany. I think I can say she'll be very, very grateful if you can bring something off, something so that the whole show can be very discreetly handled. All right, Hedge?"

"Er – "

"Good, excellent. So it's back to the field for the time being, old boy, I know you won't mind that, office work does get frustrating, don't I know it. Think up a cover story, one of course that keeps the FO right out of your background. Keep me informed, won't you, but otherwise the whole show's yours. And the very best of luck."

The Head of Security rose to his feet and reached across his desk to give Hedge the heartiest of handshakes.

It was the hour of the hairdresser: Mrs Heffer sat before a mirror, staring critically at her reflection, at the rise of the bouffant above the broad, intelligent forehead, rather lined of late since the Opposition was being more than usually tiresome and pushing. The years were beginning to catch up but Mrs Heffer was still able to push them back reasonably satisfactorily with a little help from her many bottles of creams and lotions and her indomitable will.

There was a knock at the door.

"Who is it?" Mrs Heffer shouted.

"It's me, Prime Minister."

The Foreign Secretary always announced himself as me and in any case the voice was unmistakable. Mrs Heffer clicked her tongue and shouted again. "Not now, Roly. Surely you know *that* by now."

"I'm terribly sorry, Prime Minister, but Her Majesty – "

"The Queen will have to wait," Mrs Heffer shouted. "I'll be as quick as I can."

Silence from the door indicated that the Foreign Secretary

had shifted; Mrs Heffer imagined him as a monkey with its tail between its legs and a rueful expression on its face: Roly was like that. She spoke to the hairdresser. "You'll have to hurry," she said. "I don't know *what* the Queen wants, but it could be important, I suppose." She added graciously, "We really shouldn't keep her too long."

"You said the Queen, Roly, but I don't see her."

"No, Prime Minister. Her Majesty didn't exactly come herself to see you – "

"Am I expected at the Palace?" Mrs Heffer, looking into another mirror, fluffed at her hairstyle. "I *really can't* be everywhere at once, Roly, and I'm very busy – "

"No, Prime Minister. I mean yes." Rowland Mayes was flustered, Mrs Heffer realised. "I spoke of Her Majesty only in the abstract, not as a physical presence. That's to say, I've had words with the Palace – "

"For heaven's sake, Roly, why didn't you say so?"

"I'm very sorry, Prime Minister." Rowland Mayes gave a cough and went on, "I understand the Queen is very concerned in regard to the reports about German infiltration into this country – "

"I'm sure she is," Mrs Heffer said tartly. "So am I. Well?"

Another cough. "She is particularly disturbed to learn of the Nazi, Klaus The Long Knife. But – I hope I did right, Prime Minister – I was able to reassure the – the person who telephoned – "

"The person who telephoned? Has this person got a name, Roly?"

"He didn't say, Prime Minister. I formed the impression that I was supposed to know who it was without being told."

"Well?"

"I believe it was HRH," the Foreign Secretary said.

"Oh, nonsense, Roly, he would never interfere. However, never mind that. What was this reassurance you gave?"

"Hedge, Prime Minister."

"Hedge? Is that supposed to convey something?"

"The man from the Foreign Office, Prime Minister. Security. The one who was, er, captured by the Soviets some

39

months ago and being as it were in Russian hands was able to circumvent a very nasty threat – "

"The botulism business, the reservoirs . . . and the man Logan, another Nazi? Yes, I do remember, Roly. Hedge – or wasn't it Sedge – "

"Hedge, Prime Minister."

"Hedge, then. Yes, Mr Hedge was *simply splendid*, and so very brave. So very *British*, as one would expect. What is Mr Hedge doing now?"

Rowland Mayes said, "I've been contacted by my Permanent Under-Secretary. Hedge has been put on to The Long Knife."

"Not literally, I trust."

Rowland Mayes's mouth opened in astonishment. The Prime Minister, bless her heart of course, very seldom made jokes. This one was not very good but Rowland Mayes laughed more or less heartily. "Not literally, Prime Minister. But he's considered the best man to bowl this wretched business out. I believe Her Majesty will be pleased."

"Yes indeed, and so am I. A simply splendid man. Roly, will you see to it that he is given a message. From me *personally*. I send my heartiest congratulations and am delighted to learn that he will be guarding our interests, our *British* interests, against these *wicked* men. And I shall be the first to congratulate him again afterwards. Tell him that, Roly."

"Yes, Prime Minister."

"I still don't think all this of enough *immediate* importance to interrupt my hairdresser, Roly."

Hedge was quite dizzy with conflicting emotions and with an added fear for the future, *his* future. He was being asked to do the utterly, totally impossible and he should have had the courage to say so straight away. He hadn't, and now he suffered. It was too late now to tell the H of S that Cousin Wally knew all about his Foreign Office background and was all set to make good (or bad) use of it – too late to reveal that Cousin Wally had uttered those threats, to say that Cousin Wally was expecting him to use that FO background to assist him in his nefarious schemes. And no good now saying that he'd had no idea in the world, until Shard had told him what the man from MI5 had said, that Cousin Wally was up to the sort of things he evidently was up to in regard to illegal immigrants. That part would, of course, have been the truth; but truth was now becoming a dangerous commodity. Hedge was now a double agent. That was a very nasty thought.

He went back to his office. Shard had gone and in a way that was a relief. Shard would have questioned him, impertinently, as to what had been said in the Head of Security's room, and Hedge was badly in need of time, a respite in which to formulate something. Something that would, firstly, satisfy Shard. Appease him was the word that in fact came to Hedge. Shard was very pushing, almost bullying, Hedge often felt, and he would have liked to offer him back to Scotland Yard in exchange for a more amenable and respectful man, but he knew he was stuck with him. Shard had a first-rate reputation and of course it was expected that the Foreign Office should have none but the very best. To object too strongly to Shard might even reflect upon himself.

But what was he to do now?

Perhaps he could pretend to infiltrate Cousin Wally's inner thoughts. He might be able to keep up some kind of front, knowing Wally as he did it shouldn't be too difficult to invent the thoughts that might infest his mind. But in the long run that could scarcely wash. In the end – if Wally was brought to justice – he would trip himself up and H of S would see right through him.

Sitting at his desk Hedge bit his finger-nails and his eyes grew haunted. He was deep in it now and there was no-one in whom he could confide, no-one to turn to for advice, for support. No-one at all.

Or was there?

Just one: Cousin Wally himself. Something might be worked out, some sort of bargain or compromise. It would be immensely dangerous, of course, but already he was in mortal danger and perhaps things couldn't be made worse. A visit to Stockbridge, or to the house in South Kensington, could always be ascribed to infiltration, obedience to the orders of H of S.

41

That had to be it.

Like a drowning man clutching at a straw, Hedge left the Foreign Office and once again sought out a public telephone box.

FOUR

Thinking, in connection with Shard, of appeasement, had led Hedge to think a long way back to the events leading up to 1939 and of Neville Chamberlain who had appeased Herr Hitler, not with very great success as far as Britain was concerned. And at the time Hedge was gnawing at his fingernails in the comfortable sanctity of the British Foreign Office, a man in Berlin was also thinking of appeasement and of the British who were still, even now, to a large extent anyway, addicted to the concept of appeasement in the interest of leading a quiet life. The British, who were fairly perfidious and didn't always mean what they said, had appeased their way ever since the end of the Second World War. They had appeased Stalin and Molotov and Bulganin and Kruschev. Certainly the appeasement hadn't been all that overt; there had been loud voices, angry words, a good deal of sabre-rattling, or missile-rattling, from time to time, but all that had been hot air. In the end, the Soviet Union had won out.

Until quite recently anyway, when under Gorbachev communism had taken a toss.

The man known as Klaus The Long Knife turned to his companion. The companion was a woman of a little over thirty, tall and slim, with shoulder-length black hair and a pretty face. The eyes didn't seem to fit the face: they were green, they were slit-shaped and they were as cold and hard as icebergs. The two were seated cosily in a quiet alcove in an otherwise noisy and crowded beer cellar in the Unter den Linden, now a part of reunified Berlin. The beer cellar was one much frequented by men and women whose sympathies ran alongside those of The Long Knife. In the circumstances not much talking of plans took place; unfriendly agents could lurk with their ears aflap for information. The Long Knife nudged the woman and jerked a thumb towards the exit. They got to their feet and thrust their way through the crowded cellar and climbed stone steps to the fresh air.

They walked towards the great Brandenburg Gate. In a quiet voice the man said, "Isolde, it is tomorrow."

"That you go across?"

He nodded. "Yes. As you know, I may be away for many months. You will be patient, yes?"

She looked up at him. Though tall, she was some four inches shorter than the man. "I will be patient," she said.

"For the Fatherland."

"For the Fatherland," the woman repeated. There was passion in her voice, a strangely dedicated light in the hard eyes. Germany, for so many decades split in two, had suffered a continuing degradation ever since the Treaty of Versailles that had officially ended the First World War. For a space Adolf Hitler had restored the fortunes of the Fatherland by means of his glorious Third Reich and for that space dignity had returned and the German people had been once again a proud people. But Chancellor Hitler had made his mistakes; he had underestimated the British and he had attacked the Soviet Union and the glorious Reich had collapsed in fire and widespread death with all her cities, all her great arsenals, laid in total ruin. The mistakes of the past would not be repeated. This time, when Germany was ready, the attack would be supported on a different front. And this was the purpose of the man they called The Long Knife.

"I shall send for you when I can, Isolde."

She nodded without speaking, holding tightly to his muscular arm. She would do anything for Klaus. She was very devoted; but understood well that she must always, now and for the future, play second fiddle to the Fatherland. That was acceptable, not even to be regretted. Like Klaus, she had suffered as a result of the war that had ended some fourteen years before she had been born. Both sets of grandparents

44

had been killed, the grandfathers fighting the British in the Western Desert, soldiers of Rommel's Afrika Corps of undying memory, the grandmothers in the bomb-flattened ruins of Cologne. The family fortunes had gone; everything had gone. Even though all these events were but tales told and retold by her own parents, they lived in Isolde's mind as though she had been through those terrible times herself.

She risked a question. "How long, Klaus?"

He shrugged, heaving his shoulders, like a strong bear she thought, outwardly placid but immensely dangerous. "I can't say, Isolde, how can I? The way is long . . . but changes are coming and have come already in some respects. The British are digging in their heels now. They are insisting that all of Germany remains in NATO, they have made up their minds to oppose the Russian wishes. There is an end to appeasement. As a result we shall grow very strong again. Our armies and our industries." He gave a harsh laugh. "The British will regret their insistence, but that will not be yet. All I can do is to lay the groundwork."

Again she nodded but didn't comment. The Long Knife was the leader; the New Party had boundless confidence in his abilities and in his loyalty to the cause of re-emergent Nazism, the Nazi ideals that would one day bring the German armies and the German flag to a Britain that had been well prepared, softened up in advance. They walked on, close together, passing beneath the Brandenburg Gate towards what had been Checkpoint Charlie into West Berlin. There were still British and American military police around, NATO still in evidence. No Russians now. Isolde was thinking of the next day, when The Long Knife would leave the Fatherland. He had refused to tell her where he would leave from: the less anyone knew, the safer. Those who didn't know could not reveal, even under torture. The British, Klaus had said, were capable of that.

The Long Knife, *persona non grata* in Britain and America, known to the intelligence services of both countries, left clandestinely from a small port on the estuary of the Elbe.

The Abbot of Stockbridge was at his South Kensington

45

residence. The man Oliphant, who answered Hedge's telephone call, said the boss would see him. Reverend Father in one place, Hedge thought, plain boss in the other, which seemed to epitomise Cousin Wally's two roles in life.

Half an hour after his call, Hedge was admitted by Oliphant. Oliphant smiled familiarly and said, "Hullo, ducky."

"Good afternoon, Oliphant."

"I'm not put down, you know," Oliphant said cheekily.

"I really don't care what you are. Kindly take me to Mr Crushe-Smith."

"Righty-oh, then."

The Abbot of Stockbridge was in his study, sitting at a big mahogany desk, writing. He waved at Hedge. "There you are, dear boy. What can I do for you?" He gave Hedge a conspiratorial wink. "Have you thought about what I said yesterday?"

"No," Hedge said. Then he added, "Yes."

"Make up your mind, dear boy. I would have thought it rather important, wouldn't you, that you get it right."

"It's a difficult situation for me," Hedge said.

"Yes. I see that."

Hedge glowered at his cousin. There was nothing of the abbot about Wally today. He was dressed in a business suit, pin-striped very discreetly, white shirt, gold cuff-links, very expensive silk tie. Like a successful stockbroker. Hedge's clothes were good, but they clearly hadn't cost what sat so neatly upon Cousin Wally's plump, well-fed body. It was an abomination that a man like Cousin Wally should be so well-heeled while one of the props and mainstays of the Foreign Office should be made to look and feel like the proverbial poor relation. It wasn't fair, really it wasn't.

"Well?"

"Well, what, Wally?"

"Oh, well done. Nicely alliterative I must say." Cousin Wally shot his white cuff and looked at a gold watch, one that kept itself wound by the normal movements of its owner's wrist. "I hate to hurry you, dear boy, but I've an appointment shortly. Now: is your answer yes or no?"

"Yes," Hedge said reluctantly. "Yes, it's yes."

"Oh, good. That's a relief I must say. You really can be very helpful." There was a brief pause. "Have you anything to offer at this moment, Eustace?"

"No, I haven't as it so happens. There hasn't been time. Not yet. I've been thinking over – what I should do. The yes or no."

"Quite. But not, I would have thought, a particularly hard choice. I think you do realise the alternative?"

"Yes. Yes, of course. But there's really no need for threats of that kind, you know." Hedge made an effort to sound friendly. "After all . . . we're cousins. Second cousins," he couldn't help adding.

"Yes, yes." There was a mocking grin on Cousin Wally's face. "So it's all in the family. Isn't it?"

"Yes," Hedge said, trying not to say it through set teeth.

"Yes. I'd remember that if I were you. If I were you, Eustace, I'd be damned sure never to forget it."

Hedge left the South Kensington house in a haunted frame of mind. Before being ushered out by the wretched Oliphant, he had tried to find things out, as instructed by the Head of Security. He had tried very discreetly but Cousin Wally had cut him off sharpish. Cousin Wally was saying nothing. It was Hedge's job to talk, Cousin Wally said pointedly. And talk he better had.

"Oh, yes. When there's anything to, er, talk about."

"In your job," Cousin Wally had said, "there will be." And that had been that.

Hedge walked away from the house, making towards Kensington High Street. He wanted a taxi, and two empty taxis passed him shortly after he had left the house, but he disregarded them. No connection between Cousin Wally's house and the FO must be advertised. There were no flies on Hedge. But when he picked up a taxi at last in the High Street he thought perhaps he was overreacting. After all, he was only obeying orders.

Back in his office suite he got his secretary to ring down for Shard. Shard wasn't there; his DCI was and would he do?

"It was Mr Shard I wanted," Hedge said snappishly. "Where has he gone?"

"It's understood he's gone down to Hampshire, Mr Hedge." Hedge banged the telephone down angrily. Hampshire: Stockbridge? Shard should have told him. It was very remiss. Anyway, Shard wouldn't be finding the Abbot of Stockbridge in residence. A few minutes later Hedge had a surprise. His security line from Number Ten rang. That gave him an immense shock and the blood rushed to his head in a torrent. But all was well; very well indeed. A smooth voice spoke in his ear, a man's voice. "Mr Hedge? I'm instructed by the Prime Minister to tell you how much she appreciates your readiness to serve. I don't know if you follow? Events, you know. She's really most grateful and sends her personal congratulations . . . she was much impressed by your handling of the Logan affair as well – as you know of course."

"Ah."

"Her message is, keep up the good work."

"Yes. Very gratifying. Thank you. And please be so good as to thank the Prime Minister." The call was cut. Hedge preened. It was nice to be appreciated; and the PM really was a very splendid woman indeed. It would never do to let her down. Hedge stopped preening and sat transfixed with horror. In the circumstances, what could he possibly turn out to be other than a most dreadful let-down one way or the other?

Shard drove the Volvo out for the A30 to Stockbridge. His idea was a simple recce, establish the lie of the land around the monastery and see what if anything he could pick up, discreetly, in any local pub or village store. Monasteries were usually of some sort of interest in their vicinities and probably bought at least some of their supplies locally.

Reaching Stockbridge he checked in at the Grosvenor Hotel in the main street. It was by now late afternoon; he decided that he would drive out to the monastery right away and get the geography fixed, then make his preliminary prowl after full dark.

He had no difficulty, after having made enquiries from the hotel's reception desk, in finding the monastery of God's

48

Anointed. Turning right out of the hotel, he turned right again at the western end of the village on to a road signposted for Longstock, a fairly steep climb. The country was quite well wooded in parts. The road was narrow; there was little traffic. Longstock, something over a mile from Stockbridge, was an attractive village with a number of small thatched cottages. The road continued through, very twisty thereafter and with sharp bends, and climbing, and again well wooded in parts. Shard turned north-west farther along for the villages of Abbot's Ann and Monkston. The outskirts of Abbot's Ann consisted chiefly of council houses but these gave way to more thatched cottages and an old-world village atmosphere. A steep hill led down to Monkston. Farther along, still following the directions given him in the hotel, Shard found the monastery. There were big gates standing open, and a long, winding drive. Only the roof of the building could be seen from the road. Shard drove on past, found a road off to the right that appeared to circle round behind the monastery. At the rear were thickly-growing trees, almost a forest, and once again, in one or two places, there was a glimpse of the roof. As Shard came past the back there was the sound of a bell being rung. An assembly for prayers? Or the call to the refectory maybe. Or possibly something quite different: the passing of orders to such of the temporary lay brothers who might be ready for the off, all set for infiltration into the community under new identities supplied by the Abbot. By Hedge's Cousin Wally Crushe-Smith.

The whole thing stank. Hedge was doing more than play with fire. So could he, Shard, be. It wasn't a good position to be in. What he would be doing would be, largely, saving Hedge from himself. Or trying to. As well as trying to bowl out what formed a very nasty threat to British security. And to peace.

He drove back towards Stockbridge and the hotel. Not far from the monastery he found a village pub. He stopped and went in. Driving, he kept off the hard stuff, asked for a half-pint lemonade shandy.

"New to these parts?" the landlord asked as he filled a glass. "Don't get many chancers around here. Mostly they don't leave the main roads. Spirit of adventure lacking." He grinned, matily.

Shard said yes, he was a stranger. "Business at the monastery," he said. "Or may have. I guess some of the monks'll have families in the outside world. Families they'll want to provide for."

"You're in insurance?"

Shard nodded, and named an insurance company. "Might be worth a call in the morning."

The landlord said he didn't know much about the chances of selling life insurance to monks. "Don't reckon they have any money of their own, have they?"

"Perhaps not. But – "

"I reckon they'll say God provides."

Shard laughed. "Still worth a shot. I have to live."

"Sooner you than me. I reckon they're a close-knit bunch. Close fisted with it – they don't spend much around here. Don't believe they even shop in Stockbridge. Mind you, there's money there, or I reckon there is. I've seen the boss bloke, the abbot, driving in and out. Jaguar mostly. Sometimes one of those big new Toyotas, Lexus LS 400. Other times a Range Rover. Always with the current year prefix."

Shard nodded. "Do any of the monks ever come in here?"

"Never." The landlord leaned across the bar counter. "You never see them outside the monastery, except for the abbot, driving. They grow their own vegetables, brew their own beer so it's said, and the main supplies, the groceries and that, they all come in from London. Fortnum's," he added.

"Lap of luxury?"

"That's about it. Luxury."

Another customer, a local by the look of him, came in. The landlord attended to him. Shard finished his drink, reflecting that the monasteries of old, prior to Henry VIII, had been wealthy enough. Maybe some still were, but God's Anointed didn't get their revenues in the old way. Far from it. But that had yet to be proved.

Hedge double-agented when, just as he was about to leave the Foreign Office, his internal line buzzed. The Head of

Security came on the line. "Ah, Hedge – "

"Yes, Head. I've made a preliminary contact."

"You mean – er."

"Yes." Even right inside the FO you were very circumspect. Before long they would probably give the operation a code word.

"Anything?"

"I'm sorry to say not, Head. He's keeping mum."

"Surprised to see you, after so many years?"

"Er . . . yes, very surprised."

"Natural, I suppose. No suspicions – you managed to cover up?"

"Yes," Hedge said, much relieved that the Head hadn't – yet – asked him what his cover story as to his occupation had been. "No suspicions – "

"Well, that's good, Hedge. He'll soften up, given time." There was a pause, quite a pregnant one Hedge thought. "But not too much time. This thing's dicey, very dicey. The chap – you know who I mean – he's pretty imminent." Another pause. "Butler. All right?"

"Butler," Hedge repeated in a mystified tone. Who on earth was Butler? Or did he mean Oliphant? Hedge asked just that.

"Who's Oliphant?"

"My second cousin's butler. Sort of butler anyway – "

"No, no, no! That's *what it's to be*. Don't you understand, Hedge?"

Hedge ticked over: he'd been dead right about a code name for the operation. Butler. Quite good, really: butlers looked after the silver in big houses, and cleaned the knives. The Long Knife, of course; cutler might have been too near, too obvious. Hedge said, "Yes, I do understand, Head. Yes."

"Good. Well, it's vital the chap doesn't disappear after landing. I'm relying on you, Hedge." There was a hint of steel in the voice now and this time Hedge hadn't once been addressed as 'old boy'. That was fairly indicative. Hedge said he would be doing his best and the call was cut. Hedge sat quaking. He knew he was never going to get anything at all out of Cousin Wally. And for his part the Abbot of

51

Stockbridge would soon start getting nasty. It was really a case of who got nastiest first. And Hedge would be slap in the middle.

Being unable to think of anything else to do – he'd checked the microfilm files but they were no help since the real identity of The Long Knife was totally unknown – he went home. There was still no Mrs Millington. He decided to go to his club for dinner.

Shard dined at the Grosvenor, taking his time over an excellent meal. After it, he went to the bar and sat with a half-pint of lager, reading a magazine from one of the tables. Shortly after ten p.m. he went to his bedroom, brought out an automatic from his locked briefcase, checked it, slid in a clip and put it in the pocket of his anorak. A pencil torch also went into his pocket. Then he went downstairs, round to the back of the hotel and unlocked the Volvo. He drove out of the car park, and headed towards the headquarters of Wally Crushe-Smith: he was thinking in terms of an HQ rather than a monastery, since if what Wilson of MI5 had told him was correct, the monastery aspect must be very phoney indeed.

He reached the vicinity. The night was very dark and very silent. Nothing seemed to move anywhere, except for the occasional nocturnal animal's slither or scurry. There was a feel of rain in the air, though it was not raining yet. Shard drove slowly past the big gates, still thrown open, looked along the drive as he passed but the darkness was too thick for him to see more than a few yards beyond the gates.

He drove on, going round the rear of the monastery, following the road he'd used earlier. Just off the road, well shaded by trees, was a lay-by. Shard took the Volvo into the lay-by. Switching off his engine he sat for two minutes with his driving window wound down, listening.

No sounds, nothing at all. But there was now a little wind, nothing much, and after a while he became aware of the faint sigh from overhead, the wind in the tops of the big trees. Then another sound, very faint and distant but borne along that breeze from the south-west.

Shard listened: the sound was that of digging, a spade turning the earth. And it wasn't just one spade.

Poachers? Men setting snares, or digging out badgers perhaps. Or something else?

It was worth investigating. This assignment was making Shard think in terms of dead bodies, resurrected or otherwise.

He left the Volvo, shutting the door very carefully, no slamming. He checked the automatic again, then crossed the road and moved into the trees.

A little after that midnight The Long Knife, now in his departure port on the estuary of the Elbe, also made checks of certain items of equipment as he sat in the stuffy cabin of a fishing vessel that was about to leave for the open sea. Heavy revolver; a dismantled Kalashnikov of Russian origin; two knives, long and thin and very lethal, his own preferred weapons; a Cellophane packet containing two pills even more lethal than the knives; and a small amount of Semtex explosive in a strong leather case, long and round and not unlike the cases used in the wartime British Navy for the containment of the charges that used to propel the shells from the mouths of the big guns of the cruisers and battleships of those far-off days. Similar in shape, but smaller and more easily portable.

As The Long Knife completed his checking, he felt the tremor of the vessel's engine and the movements on deck as the lines were cast off.

Getting to his feet, he looked out of the porthole. As the vessel gathered way he watched the lights of Cuxhaven fade astern. It might be a long time before he saw those lights, or any other lights of the Fatherland, again. If ever . . . there was all to gain now but there was equally all to lose. But the Fatherland stood pre-eminent, the restoration of the old glories, the noble ideals of the German Reich, and losing must not enter his thoughts other than as a spur to success. The Long Knife was not accustomed to losing, and he would not lose this time.

The fishing vessel left the Elbe estuary, heading, once clear

of the land, on a south-westerly course through the North
Sea as the British called it; The Long Knife preferred its
proper name, the German Ocean. Quite soon now, the
world might come to know it as such.

FIVE

The total dark hid Shard; his movements were cautious, his step light, he made scarcely any sound as he headed in the direction of the digging.

It grew louder.

Then it began to rain. At first Shard was unaware of the rain; the trees absorbed it. But he felt an increased dampness in the atmosphere and the sounds of digging grew a little muffled and he guessed at the fact of the rain and deduced that the digging was taking place in a clearing more immediately susceptible.

A little later he saw the loom of light ahead. A blue-shaded torch, and vague, shadowy figures, around six of them he believed, standing, or bending, in a circle. Still the digging sounds, now very obvious as such.

He moved closer.

The figures became a little clearer. He saw habits, with long tasselled girdles. Hoods were drawn over the heads of the monks, the phony monks who were making a mockery of the term monastery. Something was being buried, but what? Arms, explosives for use by Cousin Wally's associates in their mad schemes of changing the face of Britain?

Then, as the blue-shaded torch shifted its beam, Shard saw something else: a truck, into which earth was being hurled. It had been not so much digging he'd heard as earth-flinging. He saw also what looked like sheets of heavy canvas, tarpaulins. He went on watching; the loading of the truck went on beneath rain that quite soon diminished to a fine drizzle.

The blue-shaded torch swung again, lit on mounds of chalky earth.

Then the work stopped. There was some conversation that Shard was unable to catch. The tarpaulins were lifted and dragged to cover the newly dug hole in the ground, and then the truck swung round and lurched away towards where the monastery lay and behind it the monks trooped off as well.

Shard remained where he was; the monks were totally unaware of his presence. So far, so good.

He gave them fifteen minutes, playing safe. Then he came out from cover and went straight across a muddy clearing for the hole.

Hedge had dined well at his club and after dinner he sat in a very comfortable ante-room cradling a balloon glass of brandy and smoking an expensive cigar. And reflecting on many things: the wretched Abbot of Stockbridge, the Head of Security, his own terrible dilemma in respect of those two persons, and the perfidies of Mrs Millington his absent housekeeper whose sick relative was in effect costing him the price of dinner and brandy this very evening. There was just one pleasant reflection in Hedge's mind: the Prime Minister. Mrs Heffer's compliment had been very gracious indeed and had naturally increased the very great respect he felt for her. A charming woman. Mostly; she could be acerbic and was dangerous to cross. Hedge had never, of course, been close enough to her in the Establishment's hierarchy actually to cross her; he hoped devoutly that such crossing would never arise; yet, with a shiver of apprehension, knew that it was bound to. His pleasure in the PM's personal support diminished rapidly.

His various reveries were interrupted by a club servant – clubs, gentlemen's clubs, were about the last places in Britain where you still found good servants of the old sort – this particular club servant approaching with a discreet cough.

"Mr Hedge."

Hedge looked up. "Yes, Parsons?"

"Excuse me, sir. You are required on the telephone."

"Oh. Ah. Who is it, Parsons?"

"The lady didn't say, sir. Only that you were wanted urgently."

"Thank you, Parsons." Hedge got to his feet, lumbered towards the members' telephone booth. A lady. Not, surely, the Prime Minister again? No; she would scarcely be aware of his club or of his personal movements and there was no Mrs Millington at his home to tell anyone where he was. It was intriguing; but his roving thoughts came to an abrupt end when he spoke into the telephone.

"Yes? Hedge – "

"Oh, Mr Hedge. Amanda Gunning. You're wanted right away." Nothing further; the call was cut. Hedge's fingers shook as he put the handset down. Amanda Gunning – the name alone had told him exactly where he was wanted, and also why. Amanda Gunning was personal secretary to a man high up in the scale, the dangerous scale of MI5. A stringy, virginal woman of uncertain age though believed to be in her fifties, she was capable of striking fear into the hearts of men and women in very high places; she was her boss's mouthpiece. A call from Amanda Gunning could be lethal, *had* been lethal to many a hitherto hopeful career.

Hedge was agitated enough now to leave the remainder of his brandy undrunk. He sent the servant out to wave down a taxi and within five minutes was on his way to an address in Knightsbridge.

Shard looked down on the neatly spread tarpaulins. He bent and lifted the edge of one of them. He flicked on his pencil torch and beamed it down the revealed hole. He could find no bottom, but there was a ladder, a long one. A deep burial hole, ready for future use?

That seemed likely. No reasonable person would really bury arms or explosives in the ground when, in a monastery, there would surely be secure and dry places for concealment of such.

Whose bodies? More corpses like Brother Beamish way up north near Ingleborough and its cave systems?

There was nothing Shard could do currently other than report what he had found. Actually to penetrate the

Monastery of God's Anointed as a solo act would be worse than useless. He looked around: there was a track through the woods, the one the digging monks must have taken when their task was complete. It just might be worth going along that track, having a not-too-close look at the monastery's rear, since he was half-way there already. A recce was after all what he had intended.

Shard moved away from the ready-use grave and moved along the track. It was narrow, and the trees grew thickly to both sides. Twigs and branches scratched at him. He was still, he believed, some way from the monastery building when there was a commotion ahead of him.

A man came out from the forest to his left, a monk with a torch which he shone directly on to Shard.

"Oh, my! Who're you? Not another bloody poacher."

Shard kept silent. He might as well be a poacher as anything else.

The shadowy figure volunteered some information. "I'm Brother Peter, you know. Reverend Father'll want words with you. There's been too much of this sort of carry-on. Lucky I got caught short."

"Caught short?"

"Something I ate didn't agree with me. The others went on ahead. Oh, I've been ever so poorly, you wouldn't believe! The gripes. Real agony, but I'm better now. You'd best come with me."

"Really. Where to?"

"Reverend Father. The Abbot, like."

Shard acted what he had been accused of being. "Just for a bunny rabbit? Can't you turn a blind eye just this once?"

"Sorry, no. Reverend Father would do me if I did. More'n my life's worth. And it may not be just a bunny rabbit for all I know."

Shard could have seen the hole in the ground, of course. And Brother Peter was made of sterner stuff than he sounded. In the back glow from the monk's torch Shard caught the glint of steel, dull steel that formed what he believed to be a sub-machine gun. Brother Peter spoke next in un-monklike terms.

"Put your mitts in the air. Any funny tricks and I'll drill you full of bullets like a sieve." It was traditional Chicago gunman.

Cursing, Shard put his hands up. The beam of the torch travelled up and down his body. The next order came. "Move ahead of me. Take care. Don't bloody try anything, or else." Brother Peter moved aside, giving Shard clear passage past him as he stood half concealed in the trees. Shard moved, slow and cautious. Guns in the hands of those basically unaccustomed to them could sometimes be more lethal than those handled by professionals. As he drew level with Brother Peter, he dropped very suddenly to the ground and lunged sideways. Brother Peter was taken off guard. He fell.

"Oooh, you bugger," Brother Peter gasped out. The torch had flown from his hand and was beaming away somewhere in the undergrowth. Shard had his automatic out now and was covering the fallen monk in his bed of twigs and brushwood. He told Brother Peter to get to his feet, pronto.

"I can't, can I?" There was a snivel in Brother Peter's voice.

"Why not?"

"Sprained me bloody ankle, haven't I? Have to get Brother Matthew, you will. Brother Matthew's the Infirmarer."

It was something of an impasse now. Brother Peter was whimpering with pain. He would be impossible to manoeuvre back to the Volvo anonymously. And Shard was not going to put his head into a hornets' nest at this particular moment. The best thing to do would be to carry on in his role of poacher, and take the opportunity of vanishing fast. But this was not to be. Brother Peter, caught short for rather too long, was being searched for. Sounds along the track indicated the arrival of reinforcements. Five seconds later two more monks were on the scene, and both, like Brother Peter, were armed. It was some monastery.

Hedge was being put under the grill. MI5 were a very different kettle of fish from the FO's Head of Security, they made him appear an amateur. The Head of Security was a civil servant, these men were not. They were hard-faced, professional interrogators, very efficient and no respecters of persons. They had Hedge gasping for air right from the start.

"We wish you to answer questions regarding Walter Crushe-Smith, Mr Hedge."

Of course, he had guessed this; but he was unsure of his reactions. Had the Head of Security shopped him to these people, under pressure? Or had he not? Until he knew that he had to be very circumspect. MI5 could be playing cat-and-mouse with him, they were low enough for that. After due thought he repeated, "Walter Crushe-Smith?"

"Yes, Walter Crushe-Smith, Mr Hedge. What are your connections with this person?"

Panic. The dreaded moment had come. Hedge quaked; he licked his lips and by some miracle the right response came. He said hoarsely, "What makes you think I have any connections, may I ask?" The answer to that should reveal what part the Head of Security was playing, either for or against him.

But it didn't.

"We believe Walter Crushe-Smith is known to you." Known – Hedge registered the word. No mention of an actual relationship; not yet anyway. The cat-and-mouse element again? Hedge sweated. The make or break time was at hand and he would have to commit himself one way or the other.

He made up his mind: the guilty always dithered so he had to answer promptly. He said, "Really, I don't know what you mean."

"I see, Mr Hedge. Then I shall put it another way. Is Mr Crushe-Smith known to you, or is he not?"

This time, in his mounting agitation, Hedge gave the wrong answer. "No, he is not."

"Not?"

He had to stick with it now even though he had realised the enormity of his error. "Not."

"I see. You're quite, quite sure, Mr Hedge?"

They wanted him to commit himself beyond all ability to wriggle out. Hedge temporised. He put on a look of reflection and puzzlement and said, "Now you mention it . . . I do seem to recall the name. Or I think I do. Smith . . . "

"Crushe-Smith, Mr Hedge. Not an easy name, one would think, to mislay."

"So *many* Smiths . . . "

"Not so many *Crushe*-Smiths. But we do know it's familiar to you. Wilson of our lot reported the name to your man Shard."

Hedge allowed light to dawn. "Oh, yes! Yes, *that's* where I've heard it, I do remember now. Yes. Crushe-Smith. May one ask, what about him?"

"Everything about him, if you please, Mr Hedge." The bombshell was dropped, nastily. "We shall stop playing around, Mr Hedge. We happen to know that Walter Crushe-Smith is your cousin."

It had been a monumental shock even though Hedge had seen the way the wind was blowing. All those lies . . . he was now drenched in sweat. He managed to mutter, "My second cousin actually, I – "

"Don't split hairs with us, Mr Hedge." They were respect-ful to the point of the mister, but that was all now. "The matter's vital as you know very well, don't you?"

"Yes, of course I do – "

"Right, then. You'll open up fully about your cousin and your own involvement with him – "

Hedge protested, mopping at his face. "I'm *not* involved with him! Not in any way whatsoever, I do assure you. I – "

"Then why the earlier untruths, Mr Hedge?"

"Yes, I'm sorry about that. Very sorry. You see, I did hope the relationship wouldn't come out, except to my chief who in fact hoped the same. It's so very embarrassing, don't you know. But I say again . . . I have no involvement with my – my cousin."

"Very well, we accept that. For the moment." That, Hedge thought, was nasty. These fellows hadn't the trust in him that Mrs Heffer had. Besides, they were not gentlemen, they were more like sergeant-majors of the military police, very push-ing and stubborn and rude. "Now: firstly, is your cousin a man of means? Private means?"

"I really don't know. It's so long since . . . well, yes, I

61

remember there was money on his mother's side of the family. *His* family, which was not necessarily mine."

"Meaning, Mr Hedge?"

Hedge explained the relationship in detail. They didn't press on that, except to prod him as to the extent of Cousin Wally's mother's family's wealth. Hedge said again that he really didn't know but believed there could have been quite a lot since Wally's mother's grandmother on her father's side had inherited a nice competence from her husband who had been in steel. Birmingham. Involved, so Hedge believed he recalled having heard, with the Bessemers, the steel kings of nineteenth-century Birmingham. That did mean money but (according to the interrogators) perhaps not enough to run a monastery without some sort of extra financial assistance. Honest or otherwise.

The point was pressed. "Would you call your cousin an honest man, Mr Hedge?"

"I suppose so. I really don't know much about him. I've said that already."

"Yes. What are your recollections of him?"

"Recollections?"

"In childhood, let's say."

In childhood, Cousin Wally had been a stirrer up of trouble. There had been the episode of Aunt Mary's skirt; just one of many incidents that had been capitalised upon by Cousin Wally, but MI5 wouldn't be interested in all that. Hedge précis-ed his opinion of Cousin Wally. "Somewhat tiresome," he said. "Quite nasty, really."

"Be more precise, Mr Hedge. I've spoken of honesty."

Hedge said stiffly, "I believe there were occasions when, er, small sums of money disappeared from people's purses."

The MI5 man nodded. "The child is father to the man, so they say. But go on, Mr Hedge."

"I can't think of anything else."

"Try, Mr Hedge. Try very hard. Small pieces of a jigsaw puzzle . . . you know what I mean."

"Yes. But . . . well, there was an incident with a gardener's boy. Nothing to do with *honesty*, but . . . "

"Describe the incident, Mr Hedge."

"I'd really rather not."

There was a sigh from the MI5 man. "Was it sexual?"

Hedge shifted his legs uncomfortably. "Er . . . yes, it was."

"Your cousin was a homosexual?"

"I think it was just an isolated incident. He was punished and I never heard of any repetition. A boyish indiscretion, I would say."

"And in later years, Mr Hedge?"

Well, there was Oliphant, of course. Hedge thought it better to be absolutely honest where possible, so he spoke of Oliphant.

"Oliphant?"

"My cousin's butler. At his South Kensington house."

"Recently? And you know this?"

"Yes."

"But you've had no contact with your cousin – you said."

Hedge sweated. "No. Not until now. I went to his house. I was acting under orders from my chief. To, er, ingratiate myself, and – "

"Yes." There was no further comment on that aspect; they had just been trying to trip him up, but he'd seen them off over that one very nicely. The interrogator went on, "This Oliphant. Tell us about him, Mr Hedge."

"Well . . . he struck me as odd. Peculiar." They waited for him to go on; like TV interviewers, they knew the compulsion in the victim to say something further, as though it was rude not to. Hedge, as desired, went on. "He addressed me as ducky. If that's not odd, then I don't know what is."

"I take the point, Mr Hedge."

The interrogation seemed much concerned with Cousin Wally's proclivities. Hedge could understand that; there had for years been anxieties about homosexuals in high places and of course they had to take that into first account and delve. Hedge could have told them about Brother Peter at the monastery, and since he wished to keep in with MI5, he very nearly did. He just stopped himself in time. He hadn't, of course, been anywhere near Stockbridge. Not as far as MI5 was to know.

There were a lot more questions designed to extract

information about Cousin Wally's connections and friendships of years and years ago. Hedge said he really couldn't help there; they had drifted apart very early on, but he did believe that, unlike himself, Cousin Wally had not been a sticker. He had drifted from one thing to another. No, he couldn't be specific but he had once heard that Wally had dabbled with the stage. MI5 pounced on that, linking it with homosexuality, but Hedge repeated that he really didn't know. However, he risked a question.

"This man, the German, you know. The Long Knife. Is he a homosexual?"

"Bi," MI5 said, but didn't elaborate. Soon after this, Hedge was allowed to leave. Much disturbed, he took a taxi home. Soon after he got in, the telephone rang. It was Mrs Millington, very put out.

"I bin trying to get you ever so long, Mr Hedge. My sister-in-law is ever so poorly. I shan't be back inside a week, I'm sorry but there it is. I dessay you'll manage."

Hedge very much dessayed he wouldn't, but it was no use telling her. Like all so-called servants these days, Mrs Millington ran her own life. But it all put Hedge in a bad temper and he would take it out on Shard in the morning. If Shard deigned to turn up.

A file of two armed monks, with one, an older man, marching behind like the sergeant of an escort and Brother Peter hopping on one leg, took Shard on towards the monastery. The sergeant monk had a broad Australian accent and from a somewhat angry conversation Shard gathered that this Australian was a lay brother by the temporary name of Brother Werribee. He gathered also that Brother Werribee considered Brother Peter to be not only a bloody pommie poufter but simple-minded with it.

"Trust a bloody pom," he said, "to fall out for a crap in the first place. But then to bloody act like a wet bloody fish and suggest the captured bloke should go for bloody Brother Infirmarer ... wouldn't have bloody taken the chance to bugger off, would he, oh, no. And there's not much wrong with your bloody foot."

64

"I'm sorry," Brother Peter said huffily. "How, I ask you, could I – "

"Oh, bloody shut up, eh? Verbal bloody diarrhoea as well as the other sort, you are, mate."

By Shard's side, Brother Peter seemed close to tears. He muttered to himself as they went along, something about it not being fair, everyone was always on to him about something or other and he had a good mind to ask for release from his vows. Brother Werribee overheard that one.

"Vows me arse," he said, and gave a coarse laugh. "What vows you ever took, Pansy-face? An' don't get any bright ideas about Reverend bloody Father ever letting you off the hook, right?"

Brother Peter snivelled but gave no direct answer. Brother Werribee, Shard thought, had too wide a mouth for his own good. True, the atmosphere was far from monastic but Brother Werribee had now confirmed as a fact that Cousin Wally operated through the medium of fear. And another thought: whatever he, Shard, was now heading for, which wasn't likely to be anything particularly pleasant, he might in some way be able to make good use of Brother Peter who was not happy with his lot. That was at least worth bearing in mind.

They reached the back portions of the monastery. It was a vast building, once a country house on a grand scale, basement, four storeys, plus extensive attics. There was a central block and two wings, with outbuildings and what had once been a stable block and was now garages. In the centre of the rear courtyard a well stood, wooden covers in place beneath the bucket that swung from an overhead beam. Shard was taken past this and into what looked like a butler's pantry; and from here to the kitchens. Brother Peter detached himself from the escort and hopped across a stone-flagged floor to the comfort of a big wickerwork armchair with cushions, set to one side of an enormous kitchen range with four ovens and a pot of stew bubbling away on a hot-plate. Brother Peter's sub-machine gun was laid on a mat.

"Lovely," he said with a sigh, nursing his ankle. "Oh, I'm ever so *tired*, I don't know *how* I lasted – "

"Shut up, Pansy-face, and get off your bloody bum, lock the bloody door, right?"

Brother Peter did as he was told, looking huffy. As well as locking, he shot heavy bolts across the back door. Brother Werribee and the other monk, so far nameless, prodded Shard with their guns. Another door was pointed out to him and he was told to head for it.

Next morning, no Shard at the Foreign Office. Hedge, demanding Rennies, fired his guns at his personal secretary instead, finding fault with everything and not giving her a chance to say a word until he had emptied his mind of spleen.

Then she said, "Chief Inspector Bell, Mr Hedge." Bell was Shard's number two.

"What was that?"

"He asks to see you, Mr Hedge."

"Then why didn't you say so?"

"I'm sorry, Mr Hedge."

"What does he want?"

"He didn't say, Mr Hedge. Shall I send him up?"

"Yes, yes, of course, do."

Chief Inspector Bell came up. Unlike Shard, he was a man of some deference and addressed Hedge as sir.

"Well, what is it, Mr Bell?"

"Word from Customs and Excise, sir. In Shoreham, West Sussex. They took a report from the Coastguard, a boat spotted off Splash Point, in Worthing."

"Well? Was action taken?"

"It was, sir, but nothing positive emerged. The boat, a dinghy with an outboard motor, was in fact leaving the shore and contained only one man, the crew as I take it. Not being able to give a satisfactory explanation of his movements, this person was brought ashore and placed in custody in Worthing police station."

"I see," Hedge said, and asked keenly, "And?"

"Worthing police await instructions, sir. In the circumstances, if you follow me."

"I follow you," Hedge said, and added crossly, "Where's Mr Shard, do you know?"

"I don't, I'm afraid, sir. He left no instructions."

"Just like him," Hedge muttered beneath his breath. "No Mr Shard when he's wanted. Is this man being charged? And if so, what with?"

"No charge, sir, pending Whitehall instructions."

"I see. So they can't go on holding him indefinitely."

"No, sir."

Hedge's lips thinned. "Very well. I shall go myself to Worthing." Obeying his orders from the Head of Security, Hedge would go into the field. He would go to Worthing by train. No, not all the way to Worthing: he would leave the train at Shoreham and have words with Customs and Excise before going on to see the apprehended man. It was always just as well to have the background story first. And then Customs and Excise could drive him to the police station in Worthing.

Shard had been placed in a cell overnight: Brother Werribee said he would be interrogated in the morning by Reverend Father's sidekick, the precentor, Brother James.

"Don't look much like a poacher to me," Brother Werribee said. "I reckon poachers don't carry automatics." Shard's gun and torch had naturally been removed on first contact in the forest. "Don't sound like a poacher either. Or dress like one. Collar an' tie. Reckon you're not short of a bloody bunny rabbit or two, right?"

Shard shrugged. He hadn't expected the poacher angle to stand close scrutiny in any case, not beyond the simple mind of Brother Peter. But he was not saying anything and Brother Werribee, having placed him in the cell, didn't press. Nor did he linger; he locked the door and left. The cell was situated in the extensive basement area and could once have been a store-room, a small one, or a boot room or similar. The walls were obviously thick and the door was strong. There was no window and there was no light once Brother Werribee had gone and had used the switch, which was situated in the passageway running outside. The darkness enveloped Shard, thick and heavy, almost tangible. He wondered what the apartment's normal purpose was. A spare cell for visiting monks, the normal accommodation accorded the brethren of God's Anointed, or the monastic equivalent of a police or punishment cell? Before the light had gone Shard had seen a plank bed with a rather dirty blanket and beside it a kind of small cupboard, presumably for the occupant's personal possessions, the sort of receptacle that in the pre-monastic days of the great house might have contained a chamber pot. That was the total furnishing. Who would be a monk?

Shard's wrist-watch had been removed along with the handgun and torch. He had no idea, after a while, of the time. He might as well try to sleep, there being nothing else to do other than to reflect that he was now in the hot spot, the seat of Cousin Wally's religious, query, empire. If Cousin Wally came down in person, he might learn quite a lot about Hedge that he didn't know currently.

That should be interesting.

He also had a shrewd idea that he might soon come face to face with The Long Knife. That should be interesting too, if very dangerous.

Morning came, though Shard was not immediately aware of the fact. He hadn't found much sleep when the light came back on and the door of the cell was opened and Brother Peter and another monk stood in the doorway with what proved to be breakfast: a jug of water and three slices of bread, somewhat stale as he found.

"What happens next?" he asked.

Brother Peter gave a high-sounding giggle. "You'll be for it," he said. "Prying where you'd no business to be, it's a sin. Unlucky for you I was having a – was where I was. Reverend Father'll commend me for that," he added virtuously.

"I congratulate you indeed, fortuitous though it was."

"Eh? Pardon?" Brother Peter was puzzled. "Come again?"

"Oh, never mind." Shard examined the bread. "How's your stomach now?"

"Better. Oh, much better I'm glad to say. I've had a cross word or two with Brother Kitchener I can tell you. Oh, ever so cross I was." Brother Peter gestured with his hand, a brushing off motion as if swatting at a fly. "And Brother Kitchener was ever so sorry, he was really. Something was off, see, and he hadn't noticed would you believe it." Brother Peter paused. "Well, I must be off, there's work to do. Bye-bye."

A woman's work was never done, Shard thought sardonically, the phrase being one used frequently by his mother-in-law to the accompaniment of forbearing looks directed at himself. He thought now of Beth. How would she be bearing up? No news, it was said, was good news. Maybe so, but not always to a policeman's wife. Shard knew, having put his head into the lion's mouth, that he might never extract it again. Brother Peter had been farce; Reverend Father wouldn't be. Nor might the precentor be either. Cousin Wally would presumably have chosen a dependable lieutenant.

Soon after Shard had eaten his breakfast, back once again in that total darkness, the cell was opened up and the Australian tones of Brother Werribee ordered him out to face what had to be faced. And beaten.

Hedge took a taxi from Shoreham railway station to Customs and Excise. His arrival having been telephoned ahead he was surprised not to be met with transport, but there it was, Customs and Excise were not the Foreign Office and so, as in the case of the police too, what could you expect? However, he was received with proper courtesies when he reached the Custom House and so he was mollified.

He lost no time. "This man," he said. "The seafarer. What were the precise circumstances?"

They told him, in detail. The report from the coastguard had caused a full alert of the waterguard section of HM Customs and Excise and the boat had been pounced upon with no time lost, a fast customs launch having sped out from Shoreham docks to intercept.

"A thorough search, Mr Hedge."

"Of the man?"

"Of the man and the boat, Mr Hedge. Very thorough . . . drugs, you understand."

"Not presumably a long job. Not of a rowing boat."

69

The officer seemed a little hurt. "Not a very long job, no."

"And were there drugs?"

"No, Mr Hedge, boat and man were clean in that respect. Which was why our suspicions were aroused, you see."

"Ah. Suspicious, is it, when no drugs are found?"

"Yes indeed, Mr Hedge. It's drugs we normally expect to find when boats are on the move clandestinely. When you don't find drugs, then the mind leaps to other potentialities."

"Yes, I see."

"Especially at this moment in time, Mr Hedge. Without speaking of matters that shouldn't be referred to openly . . . I think you get my drift, Mr Hedge?"

"Yes. Very commendable. Now, what about the man himself? Has he been questioned?"

"Yes, Mr Hedge, but he was unable to answer our questions to our satisfaction. His English is virtually non-existent." The customs officer, who was an earnest rumpled-looking man wearing two rings of gold lace on his cuffs like a naval lieutenant, now ruffled his hair which made him look more rumpled and earnest than ever. "He answered just one question, to do with his nationality, which was clearly not British. He said he was Dutch."

Hedge raised his eyebrows. "Dutch? Why was not the Foreign Office informed of this, pray?"

"Well, to tell you the truth, Mr Hedge, I wasn't aware they had not been. In any case, I believe his claim of Dutch nationality to have been false – "

"Why is that?"

"Well, there were a lot of *neins* and *heins* and *Herrs* if you follow. *Ja* was also said, though not often. When this was reported to me, which was a while after the event, I immediately telephoned the Missions to Seamen in Littlehampton. Their opinion was that the man was probably a German national."

SIX

There had been a report from the Stockbridge area. Cousin
Wally said, "That telephone call, Oliphant."

"Oh, ah?"

"As a result of it I have to go down to the monastery. I can't
say how long for." Reverend Father, as Cousin Wally was
about to become again, gave a cheery smile. "Hold the fort,
Oliphant, old boy, won't you?"

"I'll do that."

"I know I can rely on you. Just one thing: if there are any
enquiries along . . . well, along certain lines, you know what I
mean . . . you're still not to let on that Mr Hedge has visited
this house. Understood, old boy?"

Oliphant nodded and with a duster flicked at Cousin
Wally's desk: Oliphant was very house-proud. "You're the
boss," he said.

Ten minutes later the Abbot of Stockbridge was on his way
in the Toyota Lexus LS 400 that had been spotted previously
by the innkeeper near the monastery. With him he took no
luggage: Reverend Father's suite in the monastery was always
fully equipped to receive him. Clothing, toothbrush and all.
Also all necessary weapons, nicely and handily concealed, a
home from home.

Being much worried as a result of the telephone call, for
intruders were or could be a threat, he took the drive very
fast though being prudently careful to keep mostly within the
speed limit. The Bill, if provoked, could become nosey.

The telephone call to South Kensington had been sketchy;

71

a fuller report was rendered by the precentor within minutes of Reverend Father's arrival at the monastery.

"You've not been able to find out who this man is, then?"

"No luck at all," Brother James said briefly, picking at his teeth with a matchstick. "Not that I've really tried yet . . . "

"You mean you've not roughed him up?"

"No. I thought it best to wait for you to get here, see." The Precentor of Stockbridge had once been a boxer and looked the part with his flattened nose. Legitimate boxing had ceased when jiggery-pokery behind the scenes, the fixing of fights and so on, had landed him in gaol on charges of fraud and GBH; and he was well capable of roughing up when it was expedient. He looked as though he enjoyed it. He asked, "Do right, did I, Reverend Father?"

Cousin Wally answered absently; he had been thinking hard. "Yes. Yes, quite right, Brother James. You'd better bring him in now, then we'll see."

"Give him the chop?"

"I said we'll see."

Brother James said warningly, "Don't want to take chances, not with – "

"No, indeed not, and I shall not do that, you may be sure. But before making any decisions, I shall see the man. And the chop, as you put it in your wretched prison vernacular, Brother James, may not come about. Persons are often more use alive than dead. Go and get him, if you please, Brother James."

Hedge had been delivered by Customs and Excise to Worthing police station. He was taken to the interview room and the seafarer was brought in under guard by two constables who remained standing on either side of him as he faced Hedge who was seated at a table.

"Now then," Hedge said, clearing his throat. "Do you speak English?" The formal enquiry had to be made.

It was met by a blank look.

"No English at all?"

One of the constables answered. "He doesn't seem to, sir."

Hedge grunted. How, he wondered, was he to interrogate

a man who spoke no English or, more likely he believed, didn't intend to? It was an impasse. He addressed the policeman. "Nothing found on him according to the customs people. No means of identity."

"That's correct, sir. We made our own body search, of course."

"Still nothing?"

"Nothing at all, sir."

Hedge grunted again, crossly. He was wasting his time, he felt. The seafarer looked bored, yet cheeky with it, as if he knew that his interrogator had no idea what to say or do next. Then Hedge got abruptly to his feet and announced, "He'll have to be taken to London and – and dealt with there. I'll fix that with your superintendent and the Home Office – this may turn out to be . . . not what it may appear on the surface. It may be – "

Hedge was interrupted by a sergeant who came bustling through the door into the interview room. "Mr Hedge, sir – "

"Yes?"

"A call from Whitehall." The sergeant glanced towards the suspect seafarer. "If you'd care to step outside for a moment, sir?"

Hedge got up from the table and followed the sergeant outside. "If you'd call back, sir. The Home Office. The Under-Secretary himself."

"Ah. Did he say what he wanted?"

"No, sir, he did not."

It must obviously be important, but not a great deal could be said on an open line. Hedge was accorded the privilege of the superintendent's office. He was quickly in touch with an assistant under-secretary and then, almost immediately, with the Under-Secretary of State himself.

"Hedge, Under-Secretary."

"I know that. What are you doing?"

"An interrogation, Under-Secretary – "

"The man in the boat?"

"You know about him, Under-Secretary?"

There was a snap in the voice. "Of course. Drop it, Hedge. See that he's taken under strong escort to – you'll know where. Amanda Gunning. And come yourself ... I might add that I have the authority of your own Head of Security – "

"Yes, Under-Secretary. I had already decided that the man should go to London." Hedge was determined to get that in rather than allow the Home Office to steal his thunder. He was mentally congratulating himself on his quickness of thought when the bombshell burst. The Under-Secretary asked with apparent casualness, "Does the name Crushe-Smith mean anything to you? Walter Crushe-Smith?"

"My name," Shard said, "is Jones."

Reverend Father grinned. "Smith and Jones. Very neat." He paused. "Do you follow my poor attempt at a joke, Mr Jones?"

Being officially ignorant of Cousin Wally's identity, Shard shook his head. "I'm afraid not."

"Well, never mind. What were you doing in the monastery grounds, Mr Jones? Looking for mushrooms, perhaps?"

Shard shrugged. "If you say so."

"I don't say it."

"Another joke?"

"Equally poor, Mr Jones. Come, now. You must have had a purpose, mustn't you?"

Shard, having nothing to say, said nothing. He was in a spot and he knew it. Brother James was standing close behind him and breathing heavily. Reverend Father said musingly, "People without good reasons for doing so should not go wandering about on other people's property, should they? It's not done, you know. It really isn't. Well?" The word came out like a bullet and Brother James moved in closer.

"I've nothing to tell you," Shard said. He had seen the resemblance to Hedge, but Cousin Wally was a very different character, serene, self-assured without being pompous, as hard as flint behind the stomach and the fat. He was not going to get away with his penetration of the monastery grounds. He'd thought fleetingly, but only fleetingly, of offering as a reason a need to relieve himself in the monastery's trees, but no-one with that simple but urgent need

74

would have penetrated the trees for about half a mile, being subsequently apprehended by Brother Peter well past the place where that hole in the ground had been dug.

"I think you're the Bill," Reverend Father said, almost with monklike reproof to an erring brother. "What do you say to that, h'm?"

"I'll answer that by asking a question myself. Why should you fear the Bill?"

Reverend Father smiled. "I don't, Mr Jones. I have good reason for not fearing the Bill. But if you *are* the Bill, then you'll not leave this monastery alive to tell your superiors of anything you may have seen or may yet see. In the meantime, you can be useful. Brother James?"

"I reckon 'e is the Old Bill, Reverend Father."

"I wasn't asking your opinion, Brother James. I think you know what to do now, don't you?"

Brother James was enthusiastic. "Yes, Reverend Father, that I bloody do an' all."

A man was monopolising a telephone box in Worthing's Union Place, alongside the Post Office from where he had a commanding view of the exit from the police station. He was passing a running commentary on current happenings. Customs and Excise had not been the only observer of the seafarer's departure from Splash Point. When Hermann Klein, which was the boatman's name, had been pursued and arrested, the man now in the phone box had seen and had called a number in east London. He had kept that number informed since. Now he made his final report. "Police van leaving now, motor-cycle escort. My bet's London, A24. I'll keep in touch." Leaving the box, he got into a battered-looking Nissan parked opposite, outside the Connaught Theatre. He made a fast getaway, turning left into Chapel Road, then two more left turns that took him to a roundabout just east of the police station. At this roundabout he picked up the police van with its escort and followed discreetly to four more roundabouts. When he had established that the police van and escort were definitely proceeding up the A24 he stopped at another telephone box and once again called

75

the east London number. Though the caller was unaware of this, Hedge was also aboard the van.

Shard, taken away by Brother James and another monk who had been in attendance, was duly roughed up in an above-ground cell that boasted a barred window high up in one wall. He endured the roughing up; he said nothing. Brother James, the sleeves of his habit rolled up in a businesslike way, was angry. He glared down at Shard's bloodied, swollen face.

"Don't say nothing, means you must be the Bill. Guilty conscience, see."

"You're free," Shard said with difficulty, "to form your own conclusions."

"Stands to reason." Brother James aimed a hefty kick at Shard as he lay on a bare floor. The second monk held a handgun aimed at his head. Shard winced with the pain of the kick but kept silent. Leaving his assistant behind as guard, Brother James went away. He was back within five minutes; Shard made the assumption that there had been a further consultation with Reverend Father. "On your feet," Brother James ordered.

Shard got up. With the handgun pressing into his back, he was marched away behind Brother James. He was put back in the cell which he had occupied overnight. This time, possibly as the result of an oversight, the overhead light was left on. It was better than the darkness but otherwise it brought no comfort. He wondered what the next move was going to be. He was convinced by now that the German known as The Long Knife would be somewhere in the offing. In his current situation there was nothing whatsoever he could do about it. And that hole in the ground of the night before began to assume a much more personal significance.

As a result of the Nissan driver's telephone call, certain matters were put immediately in hand from the east London number. Much use was made of the telephone; and from Leatherhead in Surrey a bunch of skinheads roared out on powerful motor-cycles, joining the A24 at the roundabout at the foot of Givons Grove. The skinheads continued south and met the police convoy on a corner, a nasty one, not far beyond the roundabout. They fanned out, blocking both carriageways. The police van braked hard. The immediate result was traffic chaos, a number of heavy shunts, a number of vehicles off the road, bodies scattered in all directions. The skinheads closed in on the back of the police van, which was already smashed in by the impact of a vehicle from behind. Two of the skinheads, using handguns, fired through into the van's interior. The seafarer from Splash Point wouldn't talk now: he died instantly, his head virtually blown from his body, while Hedge cowered in the front of the van. Then the skinheads, men with vicious faces and wearing Nazi emblems, used their guns on the policemen before mounting their machines again and, using the verges and threading through the wreckage, zoomed away, back the way they had come. The whole episode had taken little more than two minutes from start to finish.

"Very expeditiously carried out, it seems," the Head of Security said later in the Foreign Office. He had been given the reports from Scotland Yard and was passing them on in person to the Foreign Secretary. "The attackers got clean away. Of course, there's a widespread search on . . . but the Yard's not especially hopeful."

Rowland Mayes shook his head in what seemed to be disbelief. "Oh, but surely . . . a bunch of men wearing Nazi insignia – they can't hope to get away with it, can't possibly." He blinked at the Head of Security, owl-like and earnest. "Can they?"

"I'm advised they can, Foreign Secretary. Motor-cyclists with emblems are not exactly unusual. And this thing's big. They'll have any number of accomplices, any number of hideaways. No-one's going to admit anything, it'll be a blank wall for the police. And the chaos on the A24 . . . no-one seems to have got a good enough look at them. Not enough evidence for any positive identification. It was a case of sheer boldness paying off if you ask me."

"No motor-cycle numbers?"

"None," the Head of Security answered briefly. "It was a case of the chaos I mentioned. Total shock, I suppose. And a very well-executed operation. We're not up against amateurs, Foreign Secretary."

"Oh, dear. And that man, the boatman, he could have been so useful."

"Which was why he was killed, of course." The Head of Security was well aware that Rowland Mayes needed to have most things spelled out for him.

"Of course. I realise that." Rowland Mayes paused, blinking rapidly behind his glasses. "And your man? Mr Hedge?"

"In a state of shock, I understand. Been taken to hospital in Redhill."

"Oh, dear."

"Otherwise unhurt. He was lucky. He reported that a bullet grazed the sleeve of his coat."

"Well, one must be thankful for that at any rate. The Prime Minister will be relieved I'm sure."

"So very *shocking*, Roly," Mrs Heffer said, sounding savage. "So many deaths, so many people's lives upset – the injuries, you know. People are becoming totally unprincipled, don't you think, Roly?"

"Yes, indeed, Prime Minister – "

"What are you going to do about it?"

"Do about it?" Rowland Mayes's eyebrows went up quite involuntarily. "Well, Prime Minister, I really think that the police – "

"I'm not speaking of the police, Roly. I'm worried about the political implications, this *dreadful* spread of fascism, the whole democratic process coming under attack in such *appalling* ways. It's all *most* worrying, and what am I to tell the Queen?"

Rowland Mayes cleared his throat noncommittally. What the PM told the Queen was her worry, not his; but he did take the point that he was the Foreign Secretary and thus responsible for ideas imported from abroad. He cleared his throat again. "I have every confidence in Mr Hedge," he said. "I – "

"Mr Hedge, yes. I understand he was in the police vehicle. I was about to ask, how is he, Roly?"

Rowland Mayes repeated the report from the Head of

Security. "A case of shock only, and a near miss."

"Poor Mr Sedge – Hedge. So brave. So *unselfish*. Such a pity there aren't more people like Mr Sedge."

"Yes, indeed, Prime Minister." Rowland Mayes added that Hedge was currently in hospital.

"In hospital. I see. I shall go to see him, Roly, as soon as I can find the time. There's still the Queen. After that, we'll arrange a time. Or perhaps the Queen could be left a little longer. In fact she would be the *first* to understand that one simply must show one's appreciation of such loyal service."

SEVEN

Hours passed; or so Shard believed. The monastery seemed oddly silent. A pregnant sort of silence, a waiting for something to happen?

Of course the set-up was phony. But Shard would have expected a continuous façade, the so-called monks carrying out a sort of monastic routine, bells ringing for prayer or meditation, that kind of thing, and doing their allotted work, digging in the kitchen garden or whatever. But the place had almost a deserted feel about it, noticeable to Shard even in his basement cell. Not even any domestic sounds, kitchen noises, and he believed the kitchens were not far away.

It was weird.

However, explanations came eventually. There were footsteps in the passage outside and then the door was opened up. Brother Peter looked in.

"Hullo," he said, as if not expecting to see Shard.

"Good afternoon, or evening," Shard said.

"Afternoon. Some silly bugger," Brother Peter said crossly, "went and left the light on."

"I don't mind."

"I dessay not, no." Brother Peter had an automatic in his hand and had a trigger-happy look. Shard weighed the chances of a grab. The time might come if he could keep him talking, but it would be dangerous to rush things. The automatic was currently aimed at his chest and at short range even Brother Peter would be unlikely to miss.

"It's Brother Simon's job really."

"What is?" Shard asked.

"Check on lights."

"It was Brother James who put me in here."

"Yes." Brother Peter made a face. "Ooh, I do *hate* that man!"

"Brother James? I'm not surprised, but why in particular?"

"He's always on at me about something, that's why. Bloody bully! Ooh, it's lovely when he's not here, I feel quite different about things."

"Oh? What things?"

"The bloody monastery. Brother James isn't here today. Just me and Brother Paul, that's all."

"Day out?" Shard asked casually.

"Sort of, yes. Reverend Father's like that, unpredictable. Hires a coach and takes us to the seaside. It's not the seaside today, though."

"Where is it, Brother Peter?"

Brother Peter shook his head. "I'm not supposed to say. They won't take me when it's not the seaside. Reverend Father says I wouldn't appreciate it."

Shard nodded, very noncommittal. Brother Peter wasn't to be hurried. Shard sensed that he was lonely, wanted any company at all while the brethren were absent. In a moment, Brother Peter opened up a little further. "There's a place in Salisbury," he said with a touch of primness. "Massage parlour, they call it. Well, it's natural. Or I suppose it is. There being no fanny in the bloody monastery, see. They get like restive. Reverend Father likes to keep them happy."

Shard reflected that Cousin Wally probably hired a coach so that he could keep the brothers together and under firm control, no beating it for the secular world. And he could understand why Brother Peter was considered unlikely to be appreciative of the non-seaside services offered. In the meantime a little more probing might reveal more, though Brother Peter didn't strike Shard as being the sort of brother to be taken fully into Cousin Wally's confidence.

"You look tired, Brother Peter," he said with sympathy. "Why not come in and sit down? Take the weight off?"

Brother Peter tittered. "Not bloody likely! I'm not as green

81

as I'm grass-looking, you know. You'll make a grab."

"Nothing was further from my mind. And you're certainly not green."

"No?" Brother Peter seemed pathetically pleased. No doubt he got little praise in the monastery. "Do you mean that?"

"Yes." Shard paused. "You don't strike me as happy in your work, Brother Peter."

"No, I'm bloody not." Brother Peter's tone was vicious. "I bloody hate the bloody place. And you know something?"

"What?"

"You calling me Brother Peter. Respectful like. No-one else does. They're supposed to, but they don't. They talk of me in the third person if you follow. Pansy-face. That effing little pouf. Especially that Brother sodding Werribee, bloody Australian."

"Oh, dear. I'm sorry to hear that, Brother Peter."

Brother Peter gave a little clap of his hands. "There you go again, being decent. I reckon you're a decent bloke. I'm sick and tired . . . being spoken of like that. It's not bloody fair and it's not bloody *right*. Okay, so p'raps I'm a little queer, let's be perfectly open and honest. But there's no call for all them buggers to be *derogatory*, is there?"

"Certainly not. Harassment . . . there's a law against it, I believe."

Brother Peter hooted at that. "Look, mate, there's no fucking law, if you'll pardon me, in this rotten, lousy place except Reverend Father's and Brother James's." The hoot of laughter, as Brother Peter further contemplated his dreadful lot at the hands of his fellow monks, changed quite suddenly to tears. Tears of self-pity and frustration . . . Shard made sympathetic noises: the atmosphere was becoming propitious and he had a lot to learn. He said how sorry he was to hear of Brother Peter's troubles.

"Why not tell me all about it?" he suggested. "Get it off your chest. Then you'll feel a whole lot better. Troubles shared," he said tongue-in-cheek, "are troubles halved."

"Could be right at that." Brother Peter delved into the recesses of his habit and his hand came out clutching a dirty handkerchief. He wiped away his tears and managed a smile. "You're ever so *nice*," he said. Shard almost felt threatened by yet another danger.

The Long Knife, safely disembarked at Worthing's Splash Point long before the coastguard had picked up Hermann Klein's boat, which had been put into the water by a Hamburg-registered cargo vessel whilst well out of sight of the British coast, had walked away through some municipal gardens containing a putting green and flower beds. Splash Point had been chosen for his illegal entry in preference to, for instance, Littlehampton where there was a marina and a load of customs and cops who'd made drugs hauls in the recent past and would be watching carefully for yet another pounce. Worthing was not the resort of drugs pushers; Worthing, *prima donna* of the Costa Geriatrica, was full of old ladies who had never even heard of crack. In addition to which The Long Knife knew Worthing. He had first been there as a student at one of the many language schools in the town and that indeed had been what had finally cemented his loathing of the English. The inhabitants of Worthing had been unfriendly to the foreign students, accusing them of moving about in hordes and pushing the occupants of zimmer frames off the pavements into the traffic, of monopolising the buses, of vandalising the town centre, et cetera, all of this being in fact strictly true but as a good Nazi The Long Knife disregarded the strict truth in the interest of feeding his anti-British fervour. The British stank. The British must be forced to change their allegiance to something and somebody worthwhile. Mrs Heffer and democracy had had their chance and had failed.

So.

The Long Knife had no gear other than his weaponry already checked in the German port. This, and enough British currency to last until he reached his destination and the sanctuary that would be accorded him while he put his mission into effect. First was the need to get clear away from the south coast. Stealing a car could be tricky; a bicycle would do. He found one, propped in a back alley, no padlock. Very likely someone else had stolen it first and then abandoned it when it was no longer required. It was required by The Long Knife and he took it and pedalled away out of the town, reaching the A27 and the route for Chichester, turning off for Petersfield. By the time murder had been done on the A24, he was well on his way towards Winchester and Stock-bridge, looking not much like a fugitive on his anonymous bicycle in an age when fugitives sought the fastest vehicle possible. And the British police were concentrating on Splash Point back in Worthing . . .

Mrs Heffer had arrived at Redhill where Hedge had been given a bed in a cubicle and thus a little privacy though doctors and nurses tiresomely came and went and there were sundry noises off, clangs and the movement of trolleys.

The advent of the Prime Minister caused a good deal of confusion and an upset to the routine, arriving as she did at short notice in the middle of the afternoon when the senior medical staff had largely gone about their private practices. Mrs Heffer's heavily guarded car was met by the administra-tor, the medical staff being represented by a registrar.

"How is Mr Sedge?" Mrs Heffer asked anxiously.

The registrar shrugged. "Nothing wrong with him that I can find. Nerves playing up, but – "

"Shock," Mrs Heffer stated firmly, "is a serious condition." She swept into the building guided by the registrar and the senior nursing officer to where Hedge lay.

Hedge sat to attention. He had been told that Mrs Heffer was on her way and he was deeply appreciative of the ges-ture. "This is a great honour, Prime Minister."

Mrs Heffer inclined her head graciously. "The least one can do, Mr Sedge. One is so very concerned . . . one does hope you're on the road to a full recovery."

"Thank you, Prime Minister – "

"Such a terrible experience. And all those poor, innocent people who died. Really, words *cannot*, simply *cannot*, express what one feels and how much one *detests* the persons who perpetrate such vile actions."

"Quite, Prime Minister – "

"It is simply diabolical. And you have been so brave, Mr Sedge. So very brave." She gave him a winning smile and sat for a moment on the bed. Hedge shifted his feet just in time to accommodate her. Mrs Heffer waffled on about bravery and the tremendous fighting spirit of such as himself. Remembering the Queen waiting in Buckingham Palace, Mrs Heffer brought her discourse to an abrupt end, rose from the bed, shook Hedge's hand warmly, and processed back to the main entrance. Hedge was much flattered but was chagrined at being called Sedge; he hadn't liked to correct her but hoped that someone would set the record straight. After the PM had gone, Hedge's spirits sagged. There had been a euphoria about her visit but now the future loomed strongly. He had yet to report to Amanda Gunning's stronghold in Knightsbridge and be catechised again about Wally Crushe-Smith.

"That hole in the ground," Shard said.

"Nasty, ever so nasty."

"Yes."

"Fall in if you don't watch it. Of course, there's the tarpaulins."

"Yes." Shard was keeping his tone casual, just showing a polite interest, that was all. "What is it for, do you know, Brother Peter?"

"No. That is, I'm not supposed to say."

"No, of course not. I understand that. Never mind."

Brother Peter frowned, then gave an uncertain titter. "I bet you'd like to know, wouldn't you?"

Shard shrugged. "Not really. None of my business."

"I bet you'd like to know just the same."

Shard played it very carefully. He shrugged again, totally disinterested now. It was clear to him that Brother Peter couldn't wait to reveal his knowledge, wanting to surprise, astonish, shock. A ready-use grave was still Shard's theory, but he said, "I expect it's some kind of rubbish disposal. Bury the monastery's old tin cans and so on."

Brother Peter giggled and patted at his hairstyle or what was left of it after the tonsuring process. "Tisn't, you know."

"No?"

"No." Brother Peter frowned, seeming suddenly uncertain. "To be like perfectly frank and honest, I don't really understand. But it's not for old tin cans, that I do know. The lads have been set to dig down deep . . . like I said, I don't really understand, it's not my line, if you follow me."

"Exploring for oil?"

"Not that, no. Don't think it's that. They won't bloody *explain*. They just think I'm daft."

"I'm sure they don't really, Brother Peter."

"Well . . . " Brother Peter wriggled his bottom. Shard wondered if this was the moment to make a grab for the gun but, oddly, it was still being held on a steady aim for his stomach. Besides which he hadn't yet managed to get any hard information or indeed much sense out of his gaoler. Still casual, he asked if the monastery had many visitors.

"From outside like?"

Shard nodded. "Yes."

"Lay or monastic, do you mean?"

"Either."

Brother Peter thought for a while and then said, "Yes. But they don't seem to stay long."

"Oh? Why's that?"

"Ask me another. Maybe it's that Brother James. They come to meditate, see. Recharge their batteries, Reverend Father puts it. But they seem to disappear after a couple of days re-charging."

Shard wondered: into that hole, or others like it, now refilled with earth? But if Cousin Wally's financial empire was built, as it was said by Wilson of MI5 to be built, on the import of undesirable aliens, political opportunists and so on, then presumably Cousin Wally wasn't in the business of murder. But that hole still nagged at Shard. He asked again about it, still very casual.

Brother Peter gave a pout. "I said, I don't bloody know, didn't I?"

"Yes, you did. I'm sorry."

"It's all right, only don't go on about it. You was asking about visitors."

Shard said nothing.

"We get some right weird ones and all. Anyway, I call them weird. Blokes what hold services in the chapel, sort of secret."

Still Shard kept silent. It seemed the way to bring out the best in Brother Peter, who went on, "Secret like I said but, well, I did manage to find out like. Naughty me." He tittered and gave his gun-hand a smack. Shard shifted sideways; such indiscreet action could cause a tragedy. "Buggers were praising someone. Name of Hilper I think it was, but – "

"Hilper? Could it have been Hitler?"

"Could be, I dunno. Know him, do you?"

"I've heard of him."

"You a mate of his? That why you're here, is it?" There was a crafty look now in Brother Peter's eye. "Don't you say a word to Reverend Father about what I said. Or Brother James – "

"No, of course I won't," Shard said reassuringly. "And Hitler's definitely not a mate of mine. But go on."

"Music and singing," Brother Peter said reflectively. "Bloody organ full blast. I dunno . . . singing like that *Rule, Britannia* thing only it wasn't *Rule, Britannia*. More like . . . I dunno."

"*Deutschland über Alles?*"

"Yes, could be. Sounds something like what I heard, yes."

Things were coming together: German nationalism as expressed in terms of Nazism, Cousin Wally's alleged trade, The Long Knife . . . and that strange hole in the monastery grounds. There was an obvious link, but Shard was still pretty much in the dark. In any case, even if he had any hard information, it would be useless in his current situation. He turned again to Brother Peter's personal predicament vis-à-vis Brother James's bullying and the taunts of the other monks.

"Have you ever thought of relinquishing your vows, Brother Peter? I mean, you're obviously not happy with monastic life, are you?"

"No, I'm bloody not! I said that."

"So you did. Well, why not get out?"

"Huh. The chance'd be a fine thing."

"You mean there would be problems?"

"More than bloody problems, mate. Reverend Father, he'd have me balls for breakfast. It's a case of once in, never out, not if you're like on the staff, which I am. Staff as against the lay brothers, which is what some of them visitors become – "

"Are there ever any sisters, lay or otherwise?"

"No. Like I told you, no fanny. This is a Men Only establishment," Brother Peter said primly. "Which is why there's that place in Salisbury made use of. Anyway, what I was saying: some of the visitors like become lay brothers just temporary, then they sod off like the short stay mob."

"Rather confusing," Shard murmured.

"Dead right. Especially like for Brother Cellarer what manages the domestic side. *And* Brother Treasurer and Brother Kitchener. Meals and that – you know. And Brother Cellarer always on the bloody booze, talk about a piss-artist, oh my word! Once I heard him say he could drink a prodigious amount of bloody mead, and on the word prodigious he passed out like a bleeding light he did."

Shard clicked his tongue. Brother Peter was doing very well. "Do I take it you don't drink?" he asked.

"Don't touch a drop. It's a sin, see. Then there's my tummy."

"Yes, of course. Your tummy."

"Gives me hell sometimes. Like at compline."

"Complan?"

"Comp*line*. Complan's a food, didn't you know? Good stuff, I find."

"For your stomach?"

"Yes. Compline's prayers."

They were getting along like a house on fire. But time could be short. There was a need to hurry Brother Peter along, and to keep him more to the point.

Amanda Gunning came in person to Redhill, accompanied by a thick file of documents and two men from the house in Knightsbridge, neither of them known to Hedge but obviously vouched for by the simple fact of Ms Gunning's presence. One of the men was short and fat, not unlike

Hedge himself, and had a cast in one eye, which was off-putting because Hedge didn't know for certain when he was being looked at. The other man, a younger man, wore a heavy black beard, a T-shirt, jeans and sandals and carried a tape recorder. Hedge looked at him with distaste. Such a person would never be permitted in the Foreign Office but the Knightsbridge lot, except for Ms Gunning who had been at Roedean and Girton, were a pretty common bunch.

For the purposes of MI5, Hedge's bed had been shunted on its castors from the cubicle to a private room. An office, in fact, vacated by the social workers to accommodate Hedge for the time being. On the walls were various charts with ticks and crosses against a number of nursing homes and geriatric units and a calender extolling the virtues of a brand of toilet paper.

The short, fat man adjusted his cast towards, more or less, Hedge. He spoke in low tones, like a conspirator which Hedge in fact considered all MI5 operatives to be. He bent towards the bed and began his task.

"Walter Crushe-Smith, Mr Hedge."

"Yes."

"We know of the relationship. But there are consequential matters to be gone into."

Hedge palpitated beneath the bedclothes. But he was given, quite fortuitously, a breathing space for further thought. Just as the man with the cast was formulating further speech a telephone rang on one of the desks. Ms Gunning answered it. "No, I'm not Elsie. I'm sorry, but . . . " Hedge could hear a rattle like a machine-gun coming from the telephone. "Yes, this is the . . . No. I realise your anxiety but . . . " Ms Gunning's face was a study in annoyance. "This office . . . no, I've already said . . . my dear woman, I don't know anything about Doctor. Please ring off." Without waiting for the caller to do so, Ms Gunning banged down the receiver. "A patient or something," she said to the man with the cast. She had scarcely spoken when the telephone rang again. She snatched it up, said, "Doctor's on holiday," banged the instrument down for the second time and, being a woman of resource, called the hospital exchange. "No more calls to be put through until further notice," she ordered crisply. "I have Whitehall authority."

Thereafter the telephone remained silent. The exchange operators had heard all about Mrs Heffer's recent visit.

"Now, Mr Hedge. You may not be aware that a watch has been placed on Walter Crushe-Smith."

"Ah." Hedge's heart beat like a drum. "In that case . . . "

"Precisely, Mr Hedge." There was a pause while the cast steadied like a probe, or laser. Hedge had it worked out now: when the fat man appeared to be looking at a desk-top nameplate reading Elsie Sprott he was in fact looking at Hedge. "You were seen entering the house of Walter Crushe-Smith."

"Oh. Was I?"

"Yes. Also the monastery."

"Really. Well, let me tell you, Mr Whatever your name is, you haven't yet had the courtesy to tell me, that I was acting on orders received from my Head of Security in the Foreign Office. So there."

The fat man was unabashed. "Quite so, Mr Hedge. And I'm left wondering why we were not informed of this somewhat earlier."

Hedge muttered pathetically, "An oversight on the part of my chief, I dare say. I'm very sorry."

"Yes. An oversight, I see. And now I am satisfying my own wonderment for myself." The fat man leaned closer. Hedge became aware that his breath smelled nasty; he was a nasty little man, Hedge thought, and a dangerous one. "The first time you visited Walter Crushe-Smith, which was at the monastery not his house, was *before* you had received orders from your Head of Security."

Hedge remained silent. He felt as stiff as a corpse.

"And now I have to ask, Mr Hedge, what was the purpose of your visit on that first occasion?"

Hedge tried to think fast but his mind was numb. He simply couldn't get it to concentrate. He had to have time; preferably he had to consult Shard. He gave a sudden sharp bleat and clutched at his stomach, at the same time swivelling in his bed and doubling his body up in what was meant to be

90

agony. He said in a gasping voice, "The doctor, quickly. The pain . . . oh dear!"

The fat man was angry. "Oh, bugger," he muttered. "Amanda?"

Ms Gunning sprang into action. She called the exchange. It was the exchange that spoke first. "Does this mean the line's clear?"

"It does not – "

"There are three geriatric – "

"Kindly shut up and call a doctor *at once*. The social work office. And a nurse."

Brother Peter, under gentle persuasion, had grown maudlin, talking about his past. There were references to mum and dad, dad having been a coal miner (the family had lived in Yorkshire) until his occupation had been overtaken by a combination of Arthur Scargill, Mrs Thatcher and the greenhouse effect. Dad had eventually died on the dole and mum had married again. After the marriage, the stepfather hadn't wanted Brother Peter, not yet Brother at that time, around. Brother Peter had arrived at the monastery of God's Anointed by way of petty crime and an eventual prison sentence, after which he had moved south from Yorkshire, joining a party of sheepskin-clad hippies in a converted bus bound for Stonehenge. He had been picked up in Amesbury by one of the Stockbridge monks, a Brother Simon, who had bought him a cup of coffee and a bun in a cafe called The Friar Tuck which Brother-to-be Peter, being slightly dyslexic, had thought was The Triar Fuck. He had giggled at this and then one thing had led to another.

"Life's like that," he said. "I liked the monastery at first but then I got like fed up. I'd really like to be back in Yorkshire again." Brother Peter, slouched back against the doorpost, seemed to have gone into a kind of reverie, maybe seeing the dales and fells of the North, the tumbling, rock-bedded rivers and the horned sheep. Or, alternatively, the grim mills and warehouses and mean back streets of Bradford, Leeds or Huddersfield. Anyway, his concentration was going and the automatic was tending to waver. Shard tensed: the use of his leg muscles for a quick dive for Brother Peter's gun-hand, and the crashing to the floor of the monk could be a better prospect than any attempt to wean a fed-up Brother back into the world accompanied by the prisoner. The fear of Reverend Father was only too likely to keep Brother Peter rooted to the monastic life. Shard was ready for a swift spring when Brother Peter came back to life and steadied the gun once again on Shard's chest.

"Hear that, did you?" he asked.

Shard listened. He heard a distant crunch, tyres on gravel, then the squeal of brakes in need of servicing.

"That's the bus party back," Brother Peter said. He stepped backwards and banged the door shut. The bolts were pushed across from outside. Back to square one, Shard thought. With the arrival of the satisfied brethren there would have been no point in a rush on Brother Peter. Too late; and Brother Peter could still be an ally of a sort, to be preserved for future use.

EIGHT

Hedge was at home now.

The doctor, hastily summoned, had not felt inclined to suggest that a highly-placed member of the Establishment was malingering but he had raised no objections when the MI5 man had said, in an aside, that Hedge was making heavy weather of a near miss; and, with Hedge's status in mind, the consultant was summoned and Hedge was discharged. He went back to London with his inquisitors and whilst en route was forced to answer the last question asked before his relapse: what had been the purpose of his first visit to Walter-Crushe Smith?

"I can't remember."

"Oh, come now, Mr Hedge."

"I am a busy man. I have much on my mind. Do you expect me to recall each and every detail?"

"This is not exactly a detail, Mr Hedge."

Hedge breathed angrily down his nose. "I consider that it is."

"On the contrary. It is a matter of the utmost importance."

"Rubbish. In any case, I can't remember so that closes it, does it not?"

"No, Mr Hedge – "

"But if I can't remember, I can't remember, can I? Surely that's obvious? Do you expect me to trump up some sort of – of tomfool story just to satisfy you, is that it?"

"Certainly not, Mr Hedge – "

"Then kindly stop *bullying* me. I don't like it and I won't have it. One is not accustomed to this sort of thing in Her Majesty's Foreign Service and I shall put in the strongest possible complaint the moment I reach Whitehall. I shall if necessary place the matter directly before the Prime Minister herself. Mrs Heffer, in case you don't know, is very well-disposed towards me."

That shut the fat man up. Hedge savoured a moment of triumph and sat back in his seat, trying to look nonchalantly out of the window at the passing scene. The fat man, however, was not in fact shut up for very long. As the MI5 car overtook a furniture van rather fast, and Hedge was tilted against the angular form of Ms Gunning, the fat man dropped his bombshell.

"The fact that you initially concealed your relationship to Walter Crushe-Smith is seen as very relevant."

Hedge went pale and began to shake. In a high voice he said, "I have no comment at this stage."

"None is necessary, Mr Hedge. Not at this stage."

"Except one. My chief in the Foreign Office is in possession of the fact of the relationship. Just as much as you."

"Which brings us back to that first visit of yours. The visit before the fact, if I may put it that way."

A little later Hedge was deposited at his house. With instructions that he was not to leave it. A plain-clothes man would be on duty outside. Cat-and-mouse again.

Hedge felt that the end of his world had come. What would Mrs Heffer think of him now, her trust betrayed, her goodwill thrown back in her face?

The bicycle from Worthing via Petersfield and Winchester turned in that evening to the drive of the monastery, quite openly. The Long Knife pedalled on for the front door above the stone steps, dismounted and pulled at the bell-pull. The distant clang was answered by Brother Paul.

"Yes?"

"Reverend Father." The accent was guttural and commanding. "Very quick."

"Well, I don't know about quick, Reverend Father's – "

"I say again, very quick." A fist was bunched beneath

Brother Paul's nose. The fist pushed. Brother Paul gave a hoot of hurt surprise, very offended; The Long Knife pushed past and entered the monastery's plush hall. "Go now and do as you were told. Quickly."

"Oh, all *right*! Who shall I say it is?"

The man grinned, showing very white teeth. "No names. Just go."

Two minutes later The Long Knife was closeted with Reverend Father, the latter showing an unusual degree of respect and deference. "Just tell me what you want," he said, "and it'll be seen to promptly. Once the question of finance has been discussed, that is."

The Long Knife waved a heavy hand. "That is taken care of. My associates in this country will deposit two hundred and fifty thousand pounds sterling in Geneva. You will be notified when this has been done, of course."

"Yes."

"And so to what I wish. It is simple. First there is the matter of security, of safety. For me, whilst I am in the United Kingdom."

"Oh, you'll be very safe here," Reverend Father said with confidence. "No-one will – "

"I do not wish to remain here in this place. Not for very long. Here is a list." The Long Knife reached across Reverend Father's desk and took up a notepad. From a pocket he drew a biro and began writing rapidly. "It is a list of names," he said, "of persons I have to meet in secrecy. This you will please arrange soonest possible."

He finished writing and handed the list across. Reverend Father scanned it. Many of the names were those of well-known persons in politics, men and women from both sides of the political spectrum, right and left though mainly far right and far left. Reverend Father understood that; in the same way as love in the opinions of psychiatry is close to hate in the circle of human emotion, so the extremes of right and left had much in common, the operative word being dictatorship. And Reverend Father, in his role of Cousin Wally at all events, knew precisely what The Long Knife's mission was. Among the names were those of high-ranking officers of the armed forces and of the law. Other names were not familiar. Reverend Father pursed his lips. He asked, "Are all these people to give you their support?"

"No." The Long Knife uttered a harsh laugh. "Some most certainly will not. Therefore they are better, shall we say, removed from public life."

"From *public* life?"

"From life."

"Yes. I had an idea you meant that."

"And your reaction, Reverend Father?"

"Rather poor, I'm afraid. If you're suggesting I arrange for these persons to come here for your convenience, then I'm sorry I really can't oblige – "

"That is not what I want, Reverend Father. I understand the difficulty. This place would immediately be investigated if it was known that the persons had come here – "

"Quite. And of course it bloody well would be known." Reverend Father sat back in his chair, closed his eyes in thought and rested his chin on the tips of his fingers. One of the names on the list was that of Cousin Eustace Hedge, causing Cousin Wally to wonder why the Germans should bother with *him*. Another was Ms Gunning, of whom Reverend Father had heard mention in his club, which was the Athenaeum. An indiscreet remark by a somewhat inebriated MP had slipped into Cousin Wally's eavesdropping ear the information that 'the bloody Gunning woman' worked for MI5.

Cousin Wally didn't see what could be done about Ms Gunning but Cousin Eustace would be very useful in a number of ways. In the meantime, he had no intention of revealing the family connection to his visitor. He asked, "What do you wish me to do, then, in the matter of putting you in contact with these people?"

The Long Knife indicated the list, which was in two columns. "Those in the first column can be brought here at your invitation. Those are the ones who will assist. They will already know that they are to be summoned and they will not talk indiscreetly. The names in the second column are for disposal."

"Ah. Disposal – by whom?"

The Long Knife leaned forward, stared into Reverend Father's eyes. "You are known to my principals. You are trusted by them. This you know."

"Yes – "

"And they know that you have many contacts among people who can arrange such deaths. It should be very easy . . . and there is a need for speed. The time for the strike is coming fast now."

"So I'm to be the middle man?"

"Yes. For which you are being very well paid. And afterwards you will be much honoured."

"H'm." Reverend Father rubbed at his chin. The name of Hedge was in the second column, the disposal one. So were the names of Mrs Heffer and of the Leader of the Opposition.

The Long Knife said he would stay overnight and would then be on his way. He didn't say where that way would take him. (He said that in due course, no dates given, a number of other men and women would be arriving at the monastery from Germany. Reverend Father would be expected to accommodate them and at the proper time to infiltrate them into the wider world together with the necessary documents to enable them to exist officially – National Insurance, National Health, this, that and the other. This was right up Reverend Father's street, no problem at all.) And Reverend Father knew in broad outline what The Long Knife had come to achieve, which was the take-over of Britain. Just that. People in high places had already been primed up. It should be easy, according to The Long Knife. Hitler had done it. Take over the reins of power and the populace would follow like sheep. They were largely sick to death of party politics, the inevitable musical chairs of Mrs Heffer and Mr Cannock. The Long Knife's outfit would provide the thrust that the various facets of the Liberal Party and the Greens had failed to provide. The people would thereafter be happy. A *fait accompli* was always better than a lot of talk and promises about bigger retirement pensions, more hospitals and play groups and what-have-you. The people demanded positive action to break the mould, which was of itself a somewhat old-fashioned phrase now. The mould was now unbreakable. Except by The Long Knife. In his own view.

Reverend Father knew of course that the British were a different kettle of fish from the Germans. They wouldn't stomach another Hitler. But Reverend Father, with the perspicacity of Cousin Wally, didn't argue the point. There was cash to be made from both sides. All he had to do in the meantime was to humour The Long Knife and play along with him so far as it suited. He would make good use of Cousin Hedge.

And there was something, or someone, else.

Reverend Father said, "I have a man in custody. An intruder."

"Who is this person?"

"He refuses to talk. Perhaps you'd care to have a word with him?"

Hedge's telephone rang. The sound jangled at overwrought nerves and Hedge, cursing, took up the handset. It might be MI5 again, checking that he had remained inside his house as per orders. They could never leave anybody alone.

It wasn't MI5. The voice, instantly recognisable, said, "Hullo. Is that Mr Hedge?"

Oliphant. Hedge broke out into a heavy sweat. Damn Oliphant: the line was sure to be tapped and but for his thought that it might be MI5 he wouldn't have answered. He said in a high squeak, "Yes it is and I don't know who you are – "

"Come off it, ducky. Just to say you're wanted you know where. All right?"

"I don't know what you're talking about," Hedge said loudly, and banged the receiver down. Oliphant was Oliphant but he was no fool, or anyway Hedge hoped he wasn't; he would tick over, guess something was up, and not ring again.

He did ring again. Or someone did and Hedge wasn't going to risk further Oliphant. He shook with worry but let the instrument go on ringing. Eventually it stopped. Hedge poured himself a stiff shot of whisky. He reflected that it could have been just Mrs Millington with news of her sick sister-in-law. But when the phone rang again he still didn't answer. About twenty minutes later his front door bell rang. He peered down from a window; his visitors were hidden by the porch. Shaking, he went down to the hall and opened up. The fat man was there again. So was Ms Gunning.

"A few more words, Mr Hedge," the fat man said. "If we might come in."

"I suppose I've no option," Hedge said.

"You could put it that way, Mr Hedge."

Hedge led the way upstairs to his study. On arrival he saw the way Ms Gunning was looking at the whisky decanter and the half-empty tumbler and he heard her very audible sniff. The fat man wasted no time at all.

"You failed to answer the phone, Mr Hedge. Why was that?"

Hedge opened his mouth but no inspiration came. The fat man said, "Allow me to suggest why. You believed it might be the earlier caller again. The man who addressed you as ducky." There was an unpleasant intonation in the fat man's voice as he uttered the ducky. "Is this not the case, Mr Hedge? Well," he added when Hedge didn't answer, "let us assume it was, in the absence of any denial. And we would like very much indeed to know who the caller was, why you were wanted, and whereabouts you-know-where is. It might assist you if I was to reveal that our tap identified the call as coming from the house of your cousin Mr Walter Crushe-Smith. In South Kensington, that is."

There was a wealth of meaning in the tone as the fat man spoke of South Kensington. Hedge racked his brains, wondering how to explain Oliphant. He was saved too much thought when the fat man said, "Not the Stockbridge area. Which we rather think is where you-know-where is. Am I right, Mr Hedge?"

"I really don't know. You ask such confusing questions."

"Then allow me to refer you back to that telephone call," the fat man said, and added in an unfriendly tone, "ducky."

There was another sniff from Ms Gunning. It was likely enough, Hedge thought, that she acted as MI5's sniffer-out of homosexuals. Urged again by the fat man to reveal where you-know-where was and to confirm that that was where he had been bidden to by Oliphant, Hedge's resistance went into collapse.

"Yes," he said abjectly. "I really don't know why I didn't say so straight away."

"Nor do we, Mr Hedge."

"I've done my best to be helpful and – and honest with you. Indeed I've always done my best for – for the Empire, don't you know – "

"The Empire, Mr Hedge?" This time there was a snort from Ms Gunning: she had no time for dinosaurs. The fat man was smirking.

"Oh, you know what I mean," Hedge said testily.

"For Queen and Country?"

"Yes. I've done my duty."

"Quite, Mr Hedge. Now further duty awaits. We shall go to you-know-where. All three of us. This should prove interesting."

Hedge felt suddenly faint. Blood rushed to his head, overwhelmingly. He couldn't possibly arrive at the monastery in company with MI5. Cousin Wally would be wily enough to reveal things hostile to Hedge's somewhat shaky position whilst not revealing anything dangerous to himself. Cousin Wally was a rotter, a term that to Hedge conveyed everything that was ungentlemanly, selfish, dishonest and generally unpleasant. And, vis-à-vis Cousin Wally, Hedge was not exactly innocent. There was that extorted undertaking to help him by reporting things gleaned in the course of his Foreign Office duties. There was also the reverse side of that coin: the Head of Security, who had allotted him the task of working his way into Cousin Wally's confidence and reporting that way as well. A number of cleft sticks loomed, but in a sudden flash Hedge saw that the Head of Security could be made good use of in his current dilemma.

"I can't do that," he said. "Go with you to Stockbridge, I mean."

"Why is that, Mr Hedge?"

"Because my – er – cover would be blown. I've already, I think, told you that my chief has given me certain orders concerning Stockbridge. I must follow those orders. You'll surely understand that."

"There are times, Mr Hedge, when matters of national security over-ride the Foreign – "

"But for heaven's sake . . . the Head of Security *is* national security – "

The fat man brushed this aside. "And this happens to be one of those times, Mr Hedge. I must insist."

Hedge had been prodded in a sensitive area. The Foreign Office stood supreme in the Establishment hierarchy and was never to be set aside by common minions of MI5, mere jumped-up policemen and cocky with it. "If you continue to insist as you call it, I shall at once report the matter to the Permanent Under-Secretary of State, who will report it to the Foreign Secretary. The Prime Minister, whose confidence I enjoy in the *fullest* measure, will also be informed . . . and I wouldn't be in the least surprised if the two of you were suspended from duty and charged with – with blasted *treason* against the best interests of the crown and state – "

The fat man lifted a hand, soothingly. "Really, Mr Hedge, there's no need to go overboard. Naturally, I shall confirm my request with your Head of Security. This I shall do at once. If I may make use of your security telephone?"

Brother Peter had been sent down with another brother to unlock Shard's cell.

"Is this a release?" Shard asked, knowing what the answer would be.

"Reverend Father wants to see you. There's another bloke with him."

"Another brother?"

"If he is, he's lay. Don't reckon he's English. Good-looking, though. Strong with it, all muscle, lovely . . . anyway, come on out or Reverend Father'll be ever so angry and then he'll take it out on me."

Shard left the cell. Brother Peter and his mate both carried handguns and the mate looked dangerous, with a sort of crazed look in his eye. While Brother Peter led the way the other brother kept his gun pressed firmly into Shard's spine. They went along the cell passage, up some stairs to a green-baize door and through this into the hall. Thence up a wide and graceful staircase leading to what Shard took to have once been a minstrels' gallery. Off this gallery another corridor opened, a short corridor with a heavy door at its end. Brother Peter knocked at this door and was admitted. He stood aside for Shard to enter, falling in behind him with his gun at the ready.

"Done what you said, Reverend Father – "

"All right, Brother Peter. You can both go."

"Yes, Reverend Father."

"Make sure the door's locked and stand guard outside."

"Yes, Reverend Father."

The brothers turned away and left the room. Reverend Father, or Cousin Wally, appeared to be alone. But not for long. A tall, muscled man emerged from the lee of thick curtains drawn back from a big window that gave on to wooded parkland. He stood beside Reverend Father's desk, looking Shard up and down. He carried no overt weaponry but his whole aspect was threatening, blood-thirsty, the look of a born killer who enjoyed his work. Shard knew instinctively that this was the man they called Klaus The Long Knife, the man with the mission against the United Kingdom.

NINE

Hedge's submissions had paid off. Telephoned on the security line, his chief had stood by him. He had a use for Hedge and didn't want him blown to Cousin Wally. The fat man, however, had stood his ground: it was vital, for certain reasons, that Hedge should confront his cousin in the presence of MI5. They wanted, the fat man said down the phone, no worms in the woodwork.

"Meaning Mr Hedge?"

"If the cap fits, sir."

"It doesn't, and if I were you I'd watch my words."

"I'm sorry, sir, but I shall have to insist – "

"So shall I. However, to satisfy you, I shall contact the Permanent Under-Secretary of State."

It was a wordy wrangle; so wordy and protracted and eventually one conducted in such frigid tones of upset protocol and relative status, that it went, as predicted by Hedge, to the Foreign Secretary. And thence, by sheerest chance owing to the sudden and unexpected arrival of Mrs Heffer in the Foreign Office, to the Prime Minister herself.

Mrs Heffer caught the end of the telephone conversation.

"What's all this about Mr Hedge, Roly, or isn't it really Sedge?"

"Hedge, Prime Minister."

"Hedge, then. Such a *splendid* person, and that *dastardly* attack." Mrs Heffer glanced in a handy mirror behind the Foreign Secretary and patted at her hair-do before sitting down. "Well, Roly, what is it all about?"

Rowland Mayes explained in some detail: Mr Hedge was in something of a pickle. His loyalties were in doubt.

"*In doubt*, Roly?"

"Well, Prime Minister, let us say a slight cloud – "

"What utter nonsense," Mrs Heffer broke in briskly. "Not Mr Sedge – Hedge. Who says so?"

"I understand," Rowland Mayes said with diffidence, "that MI5 – "

"An unreliable bunch," Mrs Heffer stated. "*Always* looking under beds. We must *never forget* Mr Hedge's sterling work during that wretched business with Moscow – the threat of poisoned water supplies by that mad German. And talking of mad Germans," Mrs Heffer continued, changing tack a little away from Hedge, "it is because of that other mad German that I'm here." It was certainly most unusual for the mountain to come to Mahomet, Rowland Mayes reflected with a certain amount of unease. The PM normally summoned people and expected them to arrive at Number 10 even before the telephone had been put down. "The Long Knife, I mean."

"Yes, Prime Minister?"

"Has he, or has he not, arrived in this country?"

"That is not yet known, Prime Minister – "

"Why not? That man who was reported off where was it, Worthing – has there been no progress on that?"

"There is nothing known for certain, Prime Minister – "

"Then it is time there was, Roly. This wretched affair is to be given *the first priority*. The whole security of this country may be at stake. All these wretched neo-Nazis rearing their heads and making trouble, one will simply not know whom one can trust which I think is a very unsatisfactory situation and it's time it was taken seriously."

"It is being, Prime Minister, I assure you. But it's primarily a Home Office concern and – "

"Oh, fiddlesticks, Roly, don't try to wriggle out of your responsibilities." Mrs Heffer's eyes flashed. "I call that *craven*. Naturally the Home Office is concerned *within this country* and I have already made my views known. But where does this threat come from?"

"Well, Prime Minister – from Germany."

"Precisely. From Germany. From a *foreign country.*"

"The EC, Prime Minister – "

"Don't talk to me about the EC, Roly. We're *British.* And foreigners are foreigners. We expect our Foreign Secretary to act accordingly. Now: tell me again about poor Mr Sedge."

"Hedge, Prime Minister – "

"Kindly don't *contradict* me, Foreign Secretary."

Rowland Mayes gave a sigh. The Prime Minister was in an awkward mood; when displeased with him, she always addressed him as Foreign Secretary. There was in fact nothing he could do about The Long Knife so long as he was outside the country other than to try to ensure that he didn't enter. If he was already inside Britain than it really was up to the Home Office, and indeed it was the immigration people in the Home Office who should be making sure he didn't enter, and if he had entered then all that there was to be done was to find him before he fomented any nasty trouble and that again was up to the Home Office . . . Rowland Mayes's mind was in a whirl; Mrs Heffer frequently had that effect upon him, she being a congenital disturber of equilibrium. Anyway, he told her again about Hedge.

"*Of course* he mustn't accompany MI5 to this monastery," Mrs Heffer said. "I *quite* understand his point, his reluctance to be revealed to his curious cousin. It's so *obvious.* Tell your people that *no notice whatever* is to be taken of this MI5 person. Tell them at once."

"But Prime Minister – "

"*At once.*"

Once again the internal telephones became busy. Hedge was off the immediate hook. As the message was being passed, Mrs Heffer assumed a pensive look. When Rowland Mayes was freed from the telephone, she said, "Monastery, Roly."

"Monastery, Prime Minister?"

"This place at Stockbridge."

"Yes, Prime Minister?"

"It occurs to me that the assistance of the Archbishop might be of some use. What do you think, Roly?"

Rowland Mayes pursed his lips. "Well, Prime Minister, there is the security position to be considered – "

"The Archbishop is surely to be trusted?"

"Oh yes, indeed he is, of course," Rowland Mayes hastened to say. "But I fear that too many people . . . so many clergy and others in the see. And in any case I would imagine the God's Anointed people are outside the jurisdiction of Canterbury." Rowland Mayes racked his brains. "They're, well, private. Not blessed by the Church. I don't know quite how I can put it." He thought further and then came up with a splendid panacea. "Like private medicine, Prime Minister."

"As opposed to the NHS? Yes, I take your point, Roly. We'll leave the Archbishop out of it then."

Mrs Heffer was very hot on private medicine. Such a relief: to bring in the Church of England would be fatal in Rowland Mayes's view and obviously in the Home Secretary's view as well. All those bishops and deans and canons poking and prying and destroying evidence or whatever, it simply wasn't to be thought of.

Still in his own home, Hedge was informed that Mrs Heffer had come to his aid. His relief was intense and he glared triumphantly at his MI5 tormentors.

"What did I tell you?" he said.

"That's all right, Mr Hedge. We can't win every time."

"I should think not! You're not God Almighty."

"A matter of opinion, Mr Hedge. Well now, you're free to move about. Free to leave the house."

"You mean this stupid watch is being withdrawn?"

The fat man nodded. "Yes, that's right, Mr Hedge. Only I'd use caution if I were you."

This was beneath Hedge's dignity to acknowledge so he just gave an irritated grunt. MI5 departed. Ms Gunning looked absolutely furious. Hedge was left with the uncomfortable feeling that the watch was by no means withdrawn. They were still hoping to catch him out. Nevertheless, when he looked out of his window into the street he observed a man with long, dirty hair, wearing T-shirt and jeans and sandals, chuck his fag-end into the gutter, shove his copy of

The Sun into a handy litter bin, lever his back off a lamp-post, and walk away.

Possibly they were being honest. But Hedge doubted it. He went down to his garage and drove to the Foreign Office convinced that he had a tail.

In the Foreign Office he sent down for Shard.

There was no Shard.

"Still absent?" Hedge demanded.

"I'm afraid so, sir."

"Where the devil is he?"

"His current whereabouts are not known, sir."

"Oh, for heaven's sake, why not?"

"Mr Shard's movements are very often not known, sir."

Wretched police jargon. But it was true that Shard was like that. A law unto himself and keep people guessing, what a pest the man was most of the time. Hedge banged down his internal line and buzzed his secretary. He wanted coffee, strong coffee. And a couple of Rennies.

"You will tell me who you are," The Long Knife said.

"Neville Chamberlain," Shard said.

"Do not play the clever fool with me or you will suffer. Why did you come here?" The Long Knife had been given the whole story, as known, by Cousin Wally: Brother Peter's fortuitous stomach complaint leading to the capture of the intruder. "Tell me at once."

Shard shrugged. "I've nothing to say. Except that I was just curious, I suppose."

"You suppose. Curious – at night, on an ordinary road, with nothing of the building in sight? You will need to think up something more convincing than that, my friend. But before long you will speak, and you will speak the truth. I am prepared to wait for that."

"You'll wait a long time."

"I do not think so. But you sound determined. So it is plain you are no ordinary passer-by with curiosity to be satisfied. Such a person would have been wishful only to get away as fast as possible, I think. You – "

The Long Knife broke off: Reverend Father's telephone

107

had rung, the outside line. "Abbot of Stockbridge," Cousin Wally said briskly. "Oh, Oliphant," he said. "Have you – "

"I tried to get your cousin like you said. He was acting funny."

"What sort of funny, Oliphant?"

"Odd funny. Look, I'm calling from a call box and I haven't got much change. Don't you expect your cousin to come to Stockbridge, that's what I wanted to say like. Something's up."

"What is, Oliphant?"

There was a rattle and a jangle and a sort of whine followed by Oliphant's voice saying 'bugger' and then silence. The change had run out. Reverend Father looked angry and frustrated. Shard, who had heard the whole conversation because Oliphant's voice was a loud one, kept all expression out of his face. What, he wondered, was Hedge up to now? Or rather, perhaps, what was up with Hedge that was making him 'act funny'? And what was 'up' with the caller?

The Long Knife was wondering as well, it seemed. "What is funny, Herr – "

"No names if you don't mind. Just Reverend Father. It's better that way as I'm sure you'll understand. Nothing in particular is the matter. A slight hiatus, that's all."

"It is important," the German said heavily, "that I am informed fully. Please bear this in mind."

"Yes. Well, of course I do agree." Reverend Father paused. "I was expecting a visitor but he is not coming after all."

"An important visitor?"

Reverend Father waved a hand. "Oh, no. Not important."

"You are sure of this? Your manner does not support a lack of importance. Tell me, please."

Reverend Father said, "A person who is in a position to help us. There has been . . . a slight delay, that's all – "

"There is no time for delay, Herr Reverend Father. I must set matters quickly in motion, and already I am expected in the north of Britain. It is unfortunate that there is delay." The German looked at Shard. "And there is this man, whose presence indicates to me danger. Now I shall tell you what I want and you will see that it is done, Herr Reverend Father."

108

*   *   *

Later that day, after Shard had been taken back to his cell and once again locked in, a telephone message was taken in a house set remotely on a fellside in Wensleydale in North Yorkshire. It was taken by a man who looked like a farmer and whose guarded conversation consisted entirely of the word 'aye' several times repeated. When the caller had rung off the farmer dialled a number and spoke to a man whom he addressed as Arry. It was, the farmer said, to be the following night, in the early hours just before the succeeding dawn.

Arry said, "Aye."

"Pass the word, reet?"

"Aye." The farmer was not the only monosyllabic York-shireman.

That was all; at any rate in Wensleydale. Arry, who lived in Ripon, became busy. He used the telephone a number of times and when he had finished he went out, got into his car and drove towards the ruins of Fountains Abbey on the Pately Bridge road. The abbey grounds were open still and Arry, after halting at the hut where tickets were sold, drove on in and parked among a number of ducks seeking bread. Disregarding the ducks, Arry left his car and walked along-side a lake towards a place known as the Valley of the Seven Bridges. Crossing a ford where cows were drinking, he turned left along the valley, crossed the various bridges over a dried-out beck, encountering another man on the last of these bridges, a skinhead in a leather, metal-studded jacket.

"All reet?" Arry asked.

"Aye."

They went on together, no further conversation taking place. They went through a gateway into a heavily wooded area and trudged along an overgrown track until they came to what appeared to be a solid rock face. Still without speak-ing they turned to the right and ploughed through thick undergrowth beneath the rock face, going for a little over a hundred metres until they met a sharp declivity, the bank of a fairly fast-running beck. With some difficulty they de-scended the bank and let themselves down into the water, which ran knee-high. Pushing against the flow, they headed as it seemed straight into the rock itself, bending their backs to come below a great overhang and go on along a natural tunnel beneath the rock. They pushed through the water for a little more than a mile. It was deathly cold; a ledge about a foot wide ran alongside the underground stream, a ledge that stood visible in the beam of a waterproofed torch carried by the skinhead. Where the ledge widened a little the skinhead, who was in the lead, stopped and said, "Reet."

"Here, is it?"

"Aye."

They clambered out of the stream. They walked along the ledge for perhaps another hundred metres, then the skinhead, behind the strong beam of his torch, dipped through a hole that led to a wide passage – wide but with little headroom so that both had to proceed bent double. On for another long stretch of acute discomfort. Then the skinhead stopped again, reached up and pressed hard on a point of rock level with his chin. Silently, as though on well-maintained hinges, a section of the rock moved, pivoting on a natural axis. The beam of the torch cut through to reveal a vast cavern, one so big that the powerful beam showed no boundary.

It showed much else, however: the place was an armoury, a magazine of immense proportions of which any army command might well have been jealous. Stocks of explosives – Semtex, dynamite, TNT . . . huge piles of weapons, sub-machine guns, grenades, assault rifles of British Army pattern, rocket launchers and their missiles, a terrorist's dream hidden away beneath the Yorkshire fells.

Arry, not unexpectedly, was speechless.

Shard's cell was opened up. Brother Peter was there again. "I'm ever so chuffed," he said, smiling and happy.

"Why? Have you got your ticket of release?"

"Not exactly, no, but we're moving out. It's all because of you, I think. And the bloke that didn't show up when Reverend Father wanted him."

Hedge, of course. Cousin Hedge. Shard asked, "We?"

"That German, and us. You and me. Well, not just me.

Bloody Brother Werribee's coming too."

"Where are we going, Brother Peter?"

Brother Peter said reprovingly, "Naughty! Shouldn't ask that but you'll see. It's going to be ever so spooky, and what with Brother Werribee . . . still, mustn't grumble, it'll be better than the bloody monastery, where we're going."

"When do we go?"

"Right away. Here, mate, I got you this. Nicked it when Brother Kitchener'd gone for a pee." Brother Peter reached beneath his habit and brought out something greasy. "Keep you going, this will." He handed it to Shard. It was a beefburger, cold and unappetising in its covering of solidified gravy. However, Brother Peter had meant well. Shard ate the offering.

Mrs Heffer had called a meeting of the cabinet. At it, the Home Secretary was the King Pin. Law and order was under threat and the Home Secretary's sway over the Metropolitan Police was in demand. It had been, in fact, at his instigation that Mrs Heffer had summoned her cabinet at short notice. There was a good deal of anxiety in Whitehall and Mrs Heffer stressed the point. "A great country like ours, to be *put about* by some pipsqueak German. I will *not* have it," she said loudly and with the flash of battle in her eyes. "Oh, what *is* it, Roly?"

Rowland Mayes went red. "Nothing, Prime Minister." The Foreign Secretary had a bad go of piles and was shifting about on his chair like a small boy trying desperately to contain a desire to be excused. "I'm sorry, Prime Minister."

"Well, do stop *wriggling*, I find it distracting."

"Yes, Prime Minister."

"Now where was I?"

"The pipsqueak German, Prime Minister."

"Yes. The neo-Nazis, the would-be Hitlers who wish not only to establish another German Reich but also to subjugate this country by *suborning* our people from their loyalties. We must make certain they never succeed." Mrs Heffer paused, studying the impact of her words on her audience. It seemed quite satisfactory. "Home Secretary?"

"Yes, Prime Minister?"

"What do you suppose these wretched people are likely to do?"

The Home Secretary, an earnest man, considered his answer carefully. "In regard to their aims, Prime Minister?"

"For heaven's sake, Home Secretary, what else?"

"I'm sorry, Prime Minister." The Home Secretary coughed in embarrassment. Mrs Heffer, a splendid woman of course, that went without saying, liked doing most of the talking herself and it was unwise for anyone else to say too much. She mostly shot down any suggestions in any case and the feeling in the cabinet was that they were all there to be told what to do rather than to be consulted. But now it seemed as though he was expected to make some contribution, so he made it. "I think their organisation is possibly widespread, Prime Minister – "

"Yes, so do I. Well?"

"An armed insurrection must be considered as a possibility and taken into account, Prime Minister."

"Yes. One has thought about that. How would they go about it? Where would they get the arms, for instance?"

The Home Secretary considered again then said, "It is easy enough for terrorist organisations to equip themselves with arms, Prime Minister. It always has been, ever since the end of the last war. The Stern Gang in Palestine, the Mau-Mau in Kenya ... the IRA, the Bader-Meinhoff gang, all those Middle East terrorists, the Red Army Faction and so on – "

"Yes, very well, you've made your point, Rufus. And then?"

The Home Secretary looked blank. "Then, Prime Minister?"

"Yes, then," Mrs Heffer said shortly. "I do wish you would pay attention. How do they seize power?"

"Ah. Yes. Well, Prime Minister, you yourself spoke of subornment. I see that as only too likely. A number of people will have been suborned in preparation, I'm quite sure – "

"Who?"

"Well, Prime Minister ... persons in high places. In the armed services and the police, in the civil service and in local

112

administration. That sort of thing, Prime Minister."

"Yes." Mrs Heffer's expression was grim. A number of persons had been known to disagree with her from time to time. Admirals, generals, air marshals who had seen their empires crumbling in the defence cuts had made rumbling noises of discontent; Mrs Heffer saw them all too clearly as possible Nazis. Likewise the police, who were always grumbling about their pay and conditions of service; they had come up against her over something to do with their rent allowances, or was it boots, she couldn't really remember, having so much to think about. Some chief constables were an unruly lot, thinking themselves too superior – typical of people who might believe themselves to be better off under a form of Nazism. And the civil service! The civil service was always seething with discontent, though in their case the pull was to the left rather than to the right. As for the local authorities, anything was possible with them. They had bitterly (and stupidly) resented being rate-capped, had resented the Community Charge that had made them accountable to their electors, which was sheer chicanery and self-seeking as any intelligent voter ought to see. The trouble was that the voters were not intelligent, or those who failed to vote for her were not, and they as well as the nondescript bunch of mayors and chief executives and magistrates might be led into seeing neo-Nazism as being salvation. This Long Knife and his henchmen might not even need a supply of weapons. Mrs Heffer had often reflected that the voters would elect Satan himself if he promised to increase the retirement pension, lower interest rates for all except OAPs with large balances in the building societies, and offer free board and lodging on the NHS to those same OAPs . . .

"Edward?"

Edward Parker-Smeaton was the Secretary for Social Security. "Yes, Prime Minister?"

"How many old age pensioners have we?"

Parker-Smeaton gasped at an apparent *non sequitur* but answered off the cuff. "In the region of three million, Prime Minister."

"In the region?"

"Give or take a hundred or so thousand, Prime Minister. I can find out – "

"No, Edward, don't bother. Three million." Mrs Heffer looked thoughtful but offered no further comment. The cabinet went into the various ways and means of combating something that was so far so amorphous as to make the discussion one of the vaguest and least productive that Mrs Heffer had ever presided over and she left the cabinet room eventually in a foul temper, leaving Rowland Mayes with the suggestion that he could do worse than consult with Mr Sedge. Or was it, after all, Hedge? Sedge, or Hedge, might be found useful also by the Home Secretary, she said angrily.

It was early morning, not long after a fresh dawn. There had been a lot of huffing and puffing on the part of Brother Peter: he was in mufti but had his habit with him in a canvas holdall plus a blanket, a pair of wellies and a little bag of odds and ends including a pack of sandwiches.

"Brother Kitchener's specials," he said. He sounded, Shard thought, apprehensive about something or other. "Ham. Got some bangers, too, cold. Some for you an' all."

"What are the rubber boots for?" Shard asked.

Brother Peter gave his accustomed answer: "You'll see." Joined a little later by The Long Knife and Brother Werribee, in mufti like Brother Peter, and as an apparent afterthought Brother Paul and an un-named but muscular brother as well, they set off. They made towards where Shard had seen the hole dug in the ground. It was now invisible, as though filled in. Brother Werribee went ahead. Where the hole had been, Brother Werribee scraped away with his foot at the earth and revealed a concrete slab. The party was halted. Brothers Werribee and Paul, assisted by the German while Brother Peter kept Shard covered with his handgun, bent to the slab and heaved it aside, grunting and groaning and sweating with the effort. When it had been shifted, Shard saw the gaping hole, chalk lined, the ladder fixed to one side and leading down into the bottomless darkness he'd seen on first arrival.

Brother Werribee stepped on to the ladder. "You next," he

114

said to the German. Shard was ordered to follow behind, with Brother Peter in rear. Brother Paul and the muscular brother were to remain behind and put the slab back in place, a hefty job.

They climbed down in silence. Below Shard Brother Werribee switched on a torch. Shard, looking down past the German and Brother Werribee, could still see no bottom. The descent went on and on.

TEN

The long climb down ended. Brother Werribee's torch showed a more or less circular chamber, a natural space in the chalk that surrounded it. A passage, or fissure, led off from the left. The temperature was warm and very even. Aside from the chalk stratum in place of rock, Shard believed that the fissure was not unlike the cave systems of North Yorkshire, caverns and passages formed millions of years ago. A moment later, in a brief exposition to the German, Brother Werribee's Australian tones confirmed Shard's thoughts.

"The passage that we'll go along, it's a natural fissure. There's not a lot of it, but farther along it joins a fault in the earth's crust. Now, that's a real long job. If you listen, you'll hear the sound of running water. Right?"

They all listened. Shard heard the distant rush of water; so did the German, who said as much.

"What is this water?" he asked.

"Underground waterfall, mate. That's where we're heading."

"And after that?"

"We hit an underground stream." Brother Werribee said no more but moved towards the entry to the fissure, beaming his torch ahead on to the chalk sides. The German followed, then Shard with Brother Peter behind with his handgun.

The assumption had now been positively made that The Long Knife had been the man seen off Worthing and that he was now inside the United Kingdom. Mrs Heffer, immediately after her abortive conference, issued orders for a witch hunt. Certain prominent personages were to be placed under surveillance and their movements closely noted. There was to be wholesale phone-tapping by MI5. Ms Gunning was kept very busy, as was the fat man who had been balked of Hedge: Mrs Heffer had been furious again and had ordered the immediate withdrawal of the watch on Hedge. And Hedge had been summoned to the presence of the Foreign Secretary himself.

Rowland Mayes had seemed embarrassed for some reason. He told Hedge to sit down and then said that the Prime Minister herself had ordered the interview.

"The Prime Minister believes you can be of much assistance, Mr Hedge. She is of course aware of your relationship to Mr Crushe-Smith."

Hedge sweated but remained silent, waiting for more. This looked like a case of history repeating itself, but he was still fogged. Already he had been set on the trail of Cousin Wally and he really hadn't got very far. He couldn't see what else the PM might want of him.

He was soon to find out.

Rowland Mayes went on, fiddling with a silver-mounted blotter on his desk, "There has been a change of mind. On the part of the Prime Minister."

"Yes, Foreign Secretary?"

"Yes. Concerning you."

Hedge felt a constriction in his heart. A charge of some sort, to do with that original concealment of Cousin Wally? He waited in much trepidation, allayed to some extent by what the Foreign Secretary had said about Mrs Heffer believing he could be of assistance. That didn't sound too bad really but there had to be a catch and the catch might lie in the change of mind said to have taken place in Mrs Heffer's head.

It did.

Rowland Mayes continued. "Initially, the Prime Minister was set firmly against the suggestion that you should accompany MI5 to Stockbridge."

"Quite so, Foreign Secretary – "

"But she is no longer."

"Oh."

Rowland Mayes appeared to go off at a tangent. "Your man Shard, Mr Sedge. Hedge, I'm sorry. Were you aware that he had disappeared?"

"I'm aware that he seems to be missing from his office, Foreign Secretary, but that is frequently the case with Shard. Am I to understand – "

"You're aware, of course, that your cousin's monastery, and his private house, have been put under surveillance. Well, there has been a report from the officers watching." Rowland Mayes paused. "Shard's Volvo has been found abandoned close to the monastery. And watching through binoculars, MI5 report having seen Shard in the company of a number of monks and of a very tall man believed to be – "

"The German, Foreign Secretary? This Long Knife, as he's – "

"So we believe, Mr Hedge, but that's not known positively at this moment. The observed party was in the act of crossing some parkland behind the monastery. From there they entered some woodland, very thick. MI5's binoculars failed to penetrate and the party was not seen again. Not as a whole. Two habited monks returned into view without the others."

"Without Shard?"

"Yes, Mr Hedge, without your man. Now, the MI5 officers withdrew and made their report. They were instructed not to follow up – not, that is, to enter the monastery grounds. It is the government's intention to handle this in an, er, different way. If you follow me."

"I'm afraid I don't quite, Foreign Secretary."

"No. Well, then, I'll put it bluntly," Rowland Mayes got to his feet and went across his room to a cupboard. He withdrew a decanter of whisky and two crystal glasses. "You'll join me, Mr Hedge."

Hedge began to feel quite faint. Foreign Secretaries didn't ever offer whisky to subordinates in their departments without very good reason, the reason of dire need. Hedge said, "Thank you, Foreign Secretary." Rowland Mayes poured and

118

Hedge took the glass in a very shaky hand.

"Your very good health, my dear Hedge."

Hedge made some inaudible return and they drank. Rowland Mayes said, "You are yourself to be the different way, my dear Hedge."

There was rather too much, too suddenly, of 'my dear Hedge'. Hedge felt fainter. He stammered out, "Different way, Foreign Secretary?"

"As I put it just now. You are after all to go to Stockbridge. At Mrs Heffer's request."

"Request?"

"A form of words, my dear fellow."

Dear fellow now . . . and it was to be regarded as an order, in the same way as a wish expressed by Her Majesty the Queen was an order. Hedge tried a protest, one that he considered could not be ignored. "Foreign Secretary, I – I've already revealed all I know about my cousin. My *second* cousin. I would achieve no useful purpose in confronting him now. In the circumstances he would never confide anything in me – "

"Perhaps not – perhaps not. Mrs Heffer seems to think . . . well, never mind that. The decision has been made." Rowland Mayes leaned forward and spoke in a voice not far above a whisper as though Cousin Wally himself might be lurking behind the wainscot. "You are to defect, my dear Hedge. You are to join the enemy. That is, you are to appear so to do."

Hedge left the Foreign Secretary's room in a muck-sweat of fear. Mrs Heffer was expecting far too much of him, though the Foreign Secretary had made it all sound as easy as falling off a log. He was to tell Cousin Wally that because of the relationship he was now *persona non grata* and he had even been threatened with prosecution. Even if there was no prosecution, his position in the Foreign Office was under review and he could have no future in the service of Her Majesty. With his life's work broken, and with his knowledge of the German threat, he had decided to get out from under and throw himself upon the mercy of his Cousin Wally. Received

119

into the monastery (as it was hoped he would be) he was to take note of everything of interest and discover what lay behind the threat posed by The Long Knife and by Cousin Wally and how the whole affair was to be stage-managed. And then? He was, Rowland Mayes said, to report. How was he to do that?

"Simple, surely, my dear fellow? You escape."

Hedge had been too dispirited to ask the Foreign Secretary how such an escape was to be contrived. He had a strong feeling that the Foreign Secretary wouldn't have an answer in any case. Rowland Mayes brought the interview to an end by saying, "Well, my dear fellow, there's no time like the present and as you know time may be very short now. I suggest you lose not a minute."

"Very well, Foreign Secretary."

Rowland Mayes was heard to murmur something vague about the gratitude of the whole country if he could bring his mission off successfully. Mrs Heffer's faith in him was mentioned once again and Hedge believed he even caught a passing mention of the Queen.

The tremendous sound of the underground waterfall was now quite close. So was Brother Peter, who kept uttering ooohs and oh dears and was pressing himself tight against Shard as though for protection and never mind the fact that he was supposed to be on prisoner's guard duty. His mental anguish was heard by Brother Werribee, who held up the column and flashed his torch to the rear.

"You been down here before, right?"

"Yes, I – "

"Then bloody stop ooohing, bloody little pommie poufter. Want me to make a report to Reverend Father, do you?"

"No, Brother Werribee – "

"Shut yer poncy little gob, then."

Brother Peter gave a whimper but otherwise took a grip on his emotions. The torch beam shifted ahead and the forward march continued. Within the next couple of minutes they had arrived at the head of the waterfall, which, when seen at close quarters, was not as fearful as its sound had made it seem: the close confines of the fissure would have magnified it. Brother Peter, however, didn't like it at all when Brother Werribee shone his torch on to a ledge running along the fissure ahead, beside the waterfall itself. This ledge was narrow and it made a fairly sharp descent towards the foot of the waterfall to run alongside the river tumbling along beneath. Brother Peter spoke into Shard's ear. "Never been further than this I haven't."

"So you don't know what lies beyond?"

"Not really, no."

"Not really? Then you do know – "

The conversation was brought to a stop by Brother Werribee who began issuing orders. "Right, now. We take that ledge, see it, and we take it carefully. Don't want to fall in, right? I'll lead . . . formation as before. Brother Peter?"

"Yes, Brother Werribee?"

"You'll keep a good watch on the bloke, right?"

"Yes – "

"What I bloody mean, Brother Peter, is this: you don't cop out because you're dead scared for your own bloody skin. You don't turn around and bugger off. Because if you do, well, you'll regret it. Remember, I got eyes in the back of me head, right?" He spoke to the German. "Just take it steady, mate, and you'll be all right."

They moved for the ledge. Spray from the waterfall was already wetting them. As they set foot on the ledge they became drenched.

Brother Peter breathed hard down Shard's neck. After a few paces Shard felt the monk's arms going round his waist. He wondered what Brother Peter had done with his handgun. There was a strong temptation to seize the disarmed moment and plunge into the rushing river below in the hopes that it would carry him clear of Brother Werribee. The temptation didn't survive: either the German or the Australian would be sure to get him with their weaponry and even if they failed in that he would be totally lost and with no sense of what lay ahead.

The moment had not yet come.

*　　　*　　　*

The Prime Ministerial witch hunt had been very quickly put in motion. Two senior members of the government were a special target: each had been heard to say, in past unguarded moments, that the country was in a mess and it was high time for a British Hitler to rise up and instil discipline where discipline had long since vanished: in the schools, in the factories, amongst the lower classes in general. Such sentiments were relevant now and the utterers of them were very carefully watched by MI5. Shortly, a summons might come from Ms Gunning, sitting at the centre of the spider's-web of Intelligence and honing her razor-blade. A number of back-bench MPs were also under surveillance did they but know it and so were a number of civil servants, largely in the Ministry of Defence, plus certain service officers. Three provincial police chiefs were suspended very suddenly and packed off on indefinite leave, their places taken by their deputies. No reason was given and indignant protests were ignored on orders from Downing Street. Mrs Heffer was adamant and implacable. No-one was going to take over the country whilst she was holding the reins of power. She said as much to the Queen, when she demanded an audience of Her Majesty as a matter of very urgent priority.

"Such wicked people, ma'am, desperadoes who'll stop at *simply nothing* to get their way and disrupt the Emp – Commonwealth. We simply must not allow that to happen, must we? My, our, your subjects are *not to be suborned* from a way of life dear to the British heart for *simply centuries* past." Mrs Heffer paused. "You agree of course."

The Queen put a word wrong. "Of course, Mrs Heffer. But you know the European Community – "

"No, ma'am." One couldn't tell the Queen not to mention the EC in her presence, nothing so blunt, but she could still be put in her place. "The European Community is *foreign*. We're *British*. You would not wish the Commonwealth to be *degraded*." Mrs Heffer went on and on for several more minutes, advising Her Majesty that she really ought to run a toothcomb through the palace staff, and the Queen was quite unable to get another word in.

*   *   *

122

"So you've come, Cousin Eustace." Reverend Father sat behind his desk, smiling and with eyebrows raised sardonically. "What a surprise ... after you failed to turn up when I wanted you."

"I'm sorry about that," Hedge said surlily. He was feeling very ill-used. Defectors had to defect with maximum security, so the journey from London to Stockbridge had been made by no opulent chauffeur-driven staff car and by no first-class railway ticket to Winchester or Salisbury with another car laid on at the station. The journey had had to be made clandestinely even though Hedge was under orders from the highest, or second highest according to traditional royalists, in the land. Hedge had left his London home more or less by slink. He had slunk from the basement area, the door normally used by Mrs Millington when her wretched sister-in-law wasn't sick, dressed in an old tweed coat and grey worsted trousers. No hat or umbrella. He had gone to Waterloo by the underground, a detestably crowded means of travel during which, so great was the crush, he had been pressed tight against a young girl who gave a little scream and accused him of taking advantage of her and who would, she said, have slapped his face if she could only have got an arm free. Hedge, covered in confusion and totally innocent, sweated with fear (what would Mrs Heffer say?) but fortunately this being Britain no-one took any notice of the girl. Disembarking shakily and ascending the escalator he had bought his rail ticket, the value of which would eventually be refunded by the Foreign Office, and had taken an anonymous seat in the second class aboard the Winchester train. At Winchester he had slunk again, this time out of the station, in a state of disorientation and doubt, wondering what his next move should be.

One did not, presumably, defect by station taxi. One could be traced; it was bound to be put about that a senior Foreign Office man, gentleman, had vanished. That would have to be done, if only to convince Cousin Wally.

It was much too far to walk. Hedge was far from being in first-rate physical condition.

He went into the town. He visited a cafe, a rather down-market one which was safer for a defector, and ordered coffee and a biscuit. These were brought by a slatternly girl who looked like a fugitive from Stonehenge and addressed him as Dad which he didn't like but was probably quite good cover. After the coffee, he had walked along a crowded street and had happened to pass a car, a very old and dilapidated Mini, out of which a young girl got and, without pausing to lock the door, ran along the street, evidently intending not to be long since the Mini had been left on double yellow lines.

Hedge stopped and stared. Steal a car? Well, quite a defector-like thing to do, and transport was vital. Not really realising the enormity of his crime, he opened the Mini's door and got in. Hedge had heard it said that all young girl drivers shared certain things in common: they never checked the oil, they never checked the tyre pressures or the radiator water, and they always left the key in the ignition. The young girl owner of the Mini had followed the pattern and indeed had gone one further: she had left the ignition switched on.

Hedge had moved out into the traffic and insinuated himself into the one way system for the A272 to Stockbridge . . .

Cousin Wally was going on. "So you nicked a car. Naughty boy! Could be a bloody stupid boy too. You're quite sure you weren't followed?"

"Quite sure. If I had been, I'd have been arrested, presumably."

"Yes. You're right there, Cousin Eustace. Still, it was a chancy thing to do. I value my privacy, for reasons you're well enough aware of." Cousin Wally paused and readjusted his habit. "So what's new?"

"New?"

"Have you," Cousin Wally asked with forbearance, "found out anything helpful? You'll remember our bargain, naturally."

"Yes, I do."

"So?" Reverend Father studied Hedge intently. "You look distrait, Cousin Eustace. That'll never do. Tell me all, why not?"

Hedge took a deep breath and came out with it, not really believing that he would be able to carry it off but steeling himself with fantasies of the honours to come if he should succeed. He said, "I'm joining you. I've, well, defected. You see, it's come out about the – the relationship. Things have really become most awkward for me."

"Indeed?"

"Yes. *Most* awkward."

"You've been chucked out of the FO? My God," Reverend Father said, laughing heartily, "that's really rich! You, of all people, to be publicly discredited!"

"It's not funny," Hedge snapped.

"Not to you, perhaps, Cousin Eustace. I see that." Reverend Father had a rather nasty glint in his eye; a sort of gloat. "For a pompous little prig like you I don't suppose it's far short of tragedy. Having to come to me for shelter, that's – "

"I said I'd defected. That's somewhat different from coming to you for shelter. I can be useful to you – you've already made that point some days ago. I – "

"You won't be much use now you've cut your Foreign Office connections. Not, that is, as useful as before. But I suppose you do have a good deal of background knowledge, the way you people work and so on."

"Yes," Hedge said. "That's what I thought you'd find useful. And as for me . . . I'm totally disillusioned. After all my years of loyal service – to have all that thrown back in my face . . . it's really too bad." He added, "I've not been thrown out exactly. But my career's finished whatever happens. And it was on the cards that I *would* be – er – dismissed the service, of course – "

"So you decided to get out one jump ahead of the pack?"

"Yes, I – "

"And now you want," Reverend Father said, "to get back at the buggers. Very natural. Well, I can certainly make use of you, Cousin Eustace. You'll have to remember one thing, though."

"What thing?"

"A very important thing: loyalty. From now on, loyalty to me."

"Family feeling – "

"Oh, yes," Reverend Father said pleasantly. "We both

know how much family feeling there is between you and me. Allow me to make a very pertinent point. If ever I find cause to suspect your devotion to me and the cause, dear Cousin Eustace, then action will follow swiftly, and as inevitably as night follows day. Do you understand?"

"Yes, and I assure you – "

"Well, don't let's have any misunderstandings on the matter. Crystal clarity is always so much better, don't you think? Then everyone knows just where he or she stands, don't they?"

"I – "

"Disposal," Reverend Father said, "is very easy here at Stockbridge."

"Disposal?"

"Of the dead, Cousin Eustace."

"The dead?" Hedge's mouth sagged and he felt suddenly very cold, almost as if dead already. "Is that meant to be a threat, Wally, to be taken personally?"

"Yes," Reverend Father said, "but let us hope it won't come to that, shall we? And now to currently more practical concerns. Of course, you can't remain here in the monastery – not for long. Defection is defection, and you say the relationship is known. I don't want prod-noses poking about my premises. That's the first thing. Now the next." Reverend Father took up an internal telephone. He spoke into it. "Brother Chamberlain's to come up at once. A new brother joining, to be fitted with a habit." Putting down the telephone, Reverend Father turned again to his cousin. "You'll need a name," he said. "As a lay brother it won't be a saint's name. And Brother Hedge is out for obvious reasons." He frowned in thought, drumming his fingers on the desk. "Oliphant," he said after a few moments.

"Brother Oliphant? I don't think – "

"No, no, it's just that thinking of Oliphant . . . you'll be known as Brother Ducky. How's that?" Reverend Father went into a paroxysm of unkind laughter.

ELEVEN

Both waterfall and stream were negotiated in safety by all hands and Brother Peter's bravery returned just as soon as the pathway flattened out and the rush of water was contained below a steep bank. The danger, Brother Werribee said, was past. The pommie poufter could breathe easy again.

"Don't keep on calling me that," Brother Peter said, and Shard sensed, though he couldn't see, the pout that accompanied the words.

"I'll call you what I bloody please, poncy-boy."

"It's not brotherly – "

"Shut yer bloody gob."

"Bloody Australians," Brother Peter muttered into Shard's ear. "Such big he-men, though . . . I always try to make allowances like. If only he'd . . . "

"If only he'd what?"

Brother Peter giggled coyly. "Well, never mind. Everything can't be perfect, can it, in an imperfect world."

They moved on, still behind the torch. The ledge began to climb, high now above the water. It was not long after the stream had vanished altogether into some hole that a pinpoint of light was seen ahead. On they went, climbing still, no-one saying anything now. Not until they were within some twenty metres of the source of light, when Brother Werribee halted the advance and addressed them.

"The pick-up'll be ready soon as we're through. Keep yer blinkers on the bloke, Brother Poncy, and don't let him try anything, right? Don't be afraid to use your gun.

We're in remote country, no-one around to hear."

Moving ahead of the others, Brother Werribee approached the exit. When close to it, he halted and gave a low whistle. He waited for thirty seconds then repeated it, this time waiting for around ten seconds before repeating it again.

A man's head appeared, framed in the hole, silhouetted against the daylight.

"All clear, Coggan?"

"All clear, Brother, yes," an Irish voice answered.

"Transport ready? If it's not, we'll wait in cover till – "

"It's here now. You can come out, no worries." The head disappeared. Brother Werribee turned round and passed the order for the party to emerge. They did so, Brother Peter's gun now back in Shard's spine. Shard looked around into a sunny day: he had no idea of his whereabouts. No familiar landmarks; and it was as remote as Brother Werribee had said. Not a soul in sight, just high, open country swept by a slight wind from the south-west. Then Shard picked up the tank tracks furrowing a distant slope: Salisbury Plain, and a military training area? Somewhere, there would be troops. He took in the Range Rover waiting in the lee of a small hillock with scrubby trees growing, an oasis of nature left by the army's guns and tanks. Of course, Reverend Father or whoever had organised the exit from Stockbridge would have chosen a day when there was known to be no troop exercise on the programme. But Shard had a feeling that the time had now come to strike a blow for freedom. It was unfortunate that the blow had first to be struck against Brother Peter. Brother Peter was the soft underbelly of the opposition; and he was the one who had the gun ready in his hand, and Shard was in need of a gun.

The party, under the orders of Brother Werribee, was now heading for the Range Rover in single file, Brother Werribee in the lead, then The Long Knife, then Shard with Brother Peter bringing up the rear, his gun bumping Shard's spine. Taking his chance, Shard stopped dead in his tracks and bent his body forward. Uttering a shrill cry, Brother Peter seemed to catapult over the bent back and in so doing dropped the gun. Shard grabbed for it, got it in his grip and came upright. The next moment he was flat on his back and unconscious. The German had been just too smart for him and thereafter Shard was never quite certain what had hit him.

Brother Chamberlain, the monk who saw to the vestments and general clothing and accoutrements of the monastery of God's Anointed, looked precisely what he once had been: a chucker-out in a night club. Now, he surveyed Brother Ducky from head to foot, critically.

"Fat little bloke, innee? No muscle, all lard. Couldn't stand up to a fu – a flea. What a name an' all, eh?"

The Abbot clicked his tongue. "I don't want your comments, Brother Chamberlain. Just get on with the job."

"Sorry, Reverend Father." Brother Chamberlain surveyed Hedge once again, narrowing his eyes at flab. Then, from an assortment of garments which he was carrying over his arm, he selected a habit and threw it towards Hedge. "Catch," he said.

Hedge caught. "What do I do with it?" he asked.

"Well, put it on, cock, what else? Sorry, Reverend Father, should have said Brother Ducky." He gave a coarse laugh. Hedge struggled with the unfamiliar clothing and Brother Chamberlain laughed again. "Strip first, Brother Ducky. Not bare buff, just down to the underwear like, get me?"

Hedge, scarlet with embarrassment, appealed to Cousin Wally. "Do I have to?"

"Yes," Reverend Father said. "You have. And when you're kitted out you'll be tonsured."

Hedge went through the routine of joining the brotherhood. Tonsured and habited, instructed in the daily routine of the monastery and how to stand meekly before his superiors (which were everyone in the place since he was the newest entry) with his head bowed and his hands clasped in front of his body and concealed by the wide, flapping sleeves of the habit, a coarse garment that tickled, he felt that he had lost his identity. If Mrs Heffer could see him now she wouldn't even be aware that he had once been the respected Hedge of the Foreign Office, a pillar of the Establishment.

129

Now he was nothing; and he couldn't wait for the moment of escape to come. He detested being known as Brother Ducky; the name caused ribaldry amongst his fellow monks; and since the monastery was not run as Hedge believed more orthodox monasteries were run, that was, on properly disciplined lines, the ribaldry was unchecked by those who should have been in authority. For the first time since leaving school, Hedge became the butt of all, the target for bullying. Had it not been for the death threat from Cousin Wally, he would have escaped before the day was out. That was, if he could: it seemed that Cousin Wally was taking prudent precautions. A brother, a lay brother named Brother Fortescue, as tough-looking as Brother Chamberlain, kept close at all times. Orders, he'd said briefly, from Reverend Father.

Despite the lack of discipline and proper orderliness, the saying of prayers took place several times a day and during these prayer sessions Brother Ducky's whirling thoughts tended to settle down just a little and he was able to concentrate on other worries. One of them was that Cousin Wally had seemed from the start extraordinarily untroubled by having been put under surveillance by MI5. Hedge wondered why this should be.

He was soon to find out.

Shard came to in the back of the Range Rover, or to be precise on the floorboards in the back of the vehicle, which was moving, or so it felt, at breakneck speed. Feet, the feet of the German and of Brother Peter, rested on his body. As he stirred, the German said something in his own language. Brother Peter also uttered, informing Brother Werribee, who was in front with the man called Coggan, who was driving, that the prisoner was coming round.

"Watch him," Brother Werribee said. "No more bloody carelessness, right?"

"No, Brother Werribee," Brother Peter answered.

Racked with pain in his head, feeling sick to his stomach, Shard registered that the day had darkened. It was not yet night but it wasn't far off. If the Range Rover had been travelling at its current speed right through the day, they must have covered a pretty fair distance. That distance could have been in any direction, of course; but Shard's hunch was that it had been north. He still had the connection with Jervaulx Abbey in mind. The Jervaulx Resurrectionists: that had to mean something, though currently Shard's mind was a blank as to what that might be.

Night came down. The Range Rover went on, traffic sounds that Shard had noted earlier were fading out, the roads emptier now. Rain started, and the air was becoming noticeably colder: north was more and more likely. There were no stops for petrol, no stops for food. Twice, after Brother Peter had been squirming around in his seat and had at last notified Brother Werribee that he was bloody bursting, a stop had been made for relief. Shard had been brought out, almost too giddy to stand without assistance, but had seen nothing but thick woods on both sides of a road that looked like a B road. No clues as to which, or where. And certainly no chance now of a break-out even had he been fit for action.

After the second stop, another long drive through a wet and windy night. Shard had no real idea of the time: his watch had been removed back in the monastery. But at last the drive ended. It ended in an anonymous dwelling, a small farm by the look and smell, in remote country. Shard, re-moved under strong guard from the Range Rover and hustled inside, was given no chance to identify his surround-ings. But the keenness of the air and a glimpse of a dry-stone wall around a pigsty suggested the north of England pretty loudly and clearly.

In the house, which appeared to be otherwise unoccupied, a meal was ordered, Brother Peter being propelled to the kitchen regions to prepare it. Stocks, Brother Werribee said, had been got in against their arrival. Brother Peter would find everything he needed in order to produce fried eggs and bacon and fried, sliced potato. The German took over the guard duty on Shard, bringing out a knife the better to perform his duties, and starting off by presenting the weapon with its lethal point a matter of millimetres from Shard's adam's-apple.

"One move," he said harshly. "Just one move. That will

131

give the excuse. This is well understood?"

"Well understood," Shard answered.

Brother Peter came back from the kitchen quarters with a complaint. "Can't find any milk," he said.

"What d'you want bloody milk for, poncy-boy?"

Brother Peter stamped his foot. "I do wish you wouldn't call me that, it's not fair – "

"Oh, fer Chrissake! Shut yer gob. And answer the question. What d'yer want milk for?"

"There's a tin of Ovaltine. I do like a glass – "

"Go outside and find the bloody cow and bloody milk it."

Brother Peter flounced away in a temper, muttering to himself. Brother Werribee swatted at a fly that had landed nearby. The German kept his watch on Shard, all set to miss nothing whatever. No-one spoke. Cooking sounds came from the kitchen; so did an appetising smell, though Shard had no appetite. He had asked for a drink of water and this had been brought by Brother Peter. After it his mouth at least felt a little better. There was a lump like an ostrich egg on the back of his head and he was still seeing stars. The smell of frying was making him feel sicker than ever.

As Brother Peter came in with the first of the fry-up for Brother Werribee's consumption, a telephone rang stridently.

Brother Ducky had earlier been sent for by Reverend Father, an abbot now out of his habit and wearing a track suit of blue and yellow stripes. On his desk lay a stripped-down automatic assault rifle – cased, but the case had not been closed. Cousin Ducky saw a threat in the very fact that the rifle had been left for him to see.

Cousin Wally looked him up and down. "You look bloody awful but it won't be for long as it happens. Needn't have bothered to kit you out. Here." He went to a cupboard and heaved out Hedge's tweed coat, grey trousers and shirt. "Put them on," he said.

Hedge asked, "Do I take it there's been a change of plan?"

"You do. Your friends – MI5. They're not so green as they're grass-looking."

132

"Are they closing in?" Hedge asked hopefully.

"It would appear so. Two men dressed as poachers have been seen snooping around inside the perimeter."

"Oh. My man Shard," Hedge began, then stopped and went very red. What a stupid thing to say! He could find no reason why he had said it, had no idea what he had intended to add to what he'd begun. It wasn't really his fault, you couldn't blame him, he'd had a simply wretched day being every monk's butt and he was really at the end of his tether what with that and his thoughts about Mrs Heffer who was relying upon him while he was getting absolutely nowhere. Thoughts about death, too. Perhaps Cousin Wally hadn't quite heard; but Cousin Wally had.

"Your man Shard. Who, might one enquire, is he?"

"Oh . . . just my man Shard, don't you know."

"No, I don't know, dear Cousin Eustace, and I would like very much to know. So tell me, h'm?"

"He's really no-one in particular . . . "

"Just a poacher, perhaps? Hence the natural reaction?" Menace had now crept into Reverend Father's tone. "Or is he something more than that? Is he, for instance, an agent of MI5?"

"Oh no, no," Hedge said with conviction since he was now actually telling the truth. "Nothing whatever to do with MI5 I do assure you. It's really not important, you know."

"It's not? Then why mention the man, in connection, it would seem, with men dressed as poachers?"

"Oh, I really don't know, Wally — "

"Reverend Father."

Hedge stared. "What?"

"You'll address me as Reverend Father, Brother Ducky. Remember who you are."

"Oh, that's a lot of rot," Hedge said angrily. "This is no proper monastery and — "

"That may well be so," Reverend Father broke in, grinning, "but it pays dividends. Now — your man Shard. He intrigues me. I'm going to suggest that your man Shard was himself snooping round my park a day or two ago. Like a poacher. Would you say I was right, Brother Ducky?

133

Remember you've defected, your loyalties have undergone a shift, have they not? Towards me, as I've mentioned before. If I'm to trust you, you must give me reason to do so, mustn't you?"

Hedge said sulkily, "I don't know all Shard's movements, I don't check on him all the time. It's possible he took a look around here, yes."

Reverend Father nodded. "That's very interesting," he said. "You'll quite likely meet him before long, but for now that's enough about your man Shard. The current point is, we're moving out. You and me and some others – in fact the whole of the brotherhood. In plain clothes. When MI5 gets here, they'll find the place deserted and a fat lot of help they'll get from that."

Hedge said, "So everything's ready, is it?"

"Nearly. Now, I need to pick your brain, Cousin Eustace as was. There are things I need to know in regard to the way in which the government, who are certainly aware of what they believe I have in mind to do, is likely to try to circumvent me. Do you follow?"

"I think I do," Hedge answered cautiously. "You're referring to this plan to – to infiltrate persons of, shall we say, fascist outlook into places of strategic importance, and – "

"And take over the country?" Reverend Father seemed amused, Hedge thought, though he couldn't see why. "Just that?"

Hedge said, "Yes. That's what I was about to say."

"Hook, line and sinker," Reverend Father murmured, still amused. "No . . . awareness of anything else?"

"I beg your pardon . . . Reverend Father?"

"The bloody idiots can't see beyond the ends of their noses. I scarcely dared to hope . . . but it seems they've been asleep. They really believe that's all, do they?"

"So far as I'm aware, yes. Are you now saying – "

Reverend Father was laughing heartily. "It's not just that, Brother Ducky, though it's all part and parcel. Have you ever heard of a village called Hanbury?"

Hedge shook his head. "I don't think so. Why?"

"It's in Staffordshire. Heart of England. During the war, a

huge arsenal was set up underground – beneath Hanbury. Alabaster mines. It was used by the Air Ministry . . . I don't know how many tons of high explosive were stored there, about a hundred feet below the surface, but I believe it wasn't far short of five thousand. Well, one day – and no-one really knows how it happened – it all went up. The racket was heard in London, and the boffins in Geneva put it down as an earthquake. There were a lot of casualties, and that part of Staffordshire ceased to exist, the land just simply died. The government of the day made no admissions and the affair was played down."

"Really." Hedge wasn't very interested. Past history was past history.

"It's going to happen again," Reverend Father said in a conversational tone. "There's a similar arsenal in North Yorkshire. They've made use of some of the deep cave systems, you know – "

"Candleby!"

Reverend Father nodded. "I see you've heard of it." Hedge had, peripherally. He believed that around ten thousand tons of high explosives had been stored deep below the North Yorkshire fells after the massive troop cuts and the start of the phased withdrawal from BAOR. He recalled the local fuss, the strenuous objections and the summary way in which those objections had been over-ruled. Scattered communities, the local people had been called, just isolated farms here and there and plenty of sheep. There was literally nowhere else as suitable for the purpose. But if that lot was to blow up . . . Hedge let out a long breath.

"Why?" he asked.

"As I said, it's all part and parcel."

"I don't follow," Hedge said, beginning to shake. He had, it seemed defected into more than he had bargained for, more than the Foreign Secretary had bargained for when he had sent him into the field. More, presumably, than even Mrs Heffer had bargained for. "Part and parcel of the take-over, do you mean?"

"Brilliantly deduced, my dear chap. And now you're part of it, dear Cousin Eustace, at least as far as the spilling of relevant beans is concerned. Oh, and by the way . . . there's something else."

"What?" Hedge asked, fearful of the answer.

"There's been more local protest – I dare say you know that. The farmers are dead worried that something could go wrong, not knowing, of course, that something *is* going to go rather nastily wrong. So there's to be a visit of investigation and reassurance by the brass. It's when the brass gets there that we go into action. It's all planned down to the last detail. Except one. We don't yet know the time and date of the visit, not that we're worried. We'll be ready whenever it's to be."

"I see." Fear was now rising fast in Hedge: he might be required to be present for all he knew. "Who's the brass?"

"Oh, the usual bigwigs. Defence Secretary, Home Secretary, Minister for the Army. Chief of the General Staff. And Mrs Heffer."

TWELVE

Brother Werribee took the call in the northern farmhouse. Ringing off, he said, "Reverend Father. Coming up, they all are. With a Brother Ducky and who the bloody hell that might be I don't bloody know. But there's a warning about you, cobber."

The last remark had been addressed to Shard, who was lying on the floor of what looked like the farm sitting-room, now with his wrists and ankles firmly roped. "Seems you c'd be this Brother Ducky's man. Right, is that?"

"Who's Brother Ducky?" Shard asked blankly.

"Dunno. Though I reckon you do. But – name of Shard. You?"

Shard met the Australian's eye. If his name was known, there was no real point in a denial. He said, "Yes." By inference, he decided, Brother Ducky must be Hedge, but what was Hedge doing in Stockbridge, in the monastery?

Brother Werribee said, "Give, right?"

Shard shrugged. "I've nothing to give."

"No? Who are you, for a start? Apart from the name."

So that hadn't emerged. Not yet. Shard wasn't going to help the process. Time might be on either side but he was going to cling to a hope that it was on his. He repeated that he had nothing to say, and at that Klaus The Long Knife came across, fingering his namesake.

He said, "A little of the persuasion, Brother Werribee?"

Brother Werribee pondered but then shook his head. "No, let it ride, we'll find out when Reverend Father gets here.

Reverend Father, he didn't say nothing about roughing the bloke up."

The German seemed disappointed. He said, "I think Reverend Father is a little, what you would say, soft?"

"Not what I think," Brother Werribee said. "We'll wait till he gets here."

"As you say, then." Klaus paused, looking down with dislike at Shard. In the German's book a little roughing up never came amiss. "When do you expect contact with Fountains?"

"Just as soon as Harry's ready. Not before."

"Yes. And when will that be, Brother Werribee?"

"Dunno. Just wait and bloody see, right? Reverend Father, he's not the one to rush anything. We have to wait to know when the nobs are coming, that's the first thing."

Brother Peter came in with the rest of supper. "Super fry-up," he announced, putting the plates on a table in the middle of the room. He looked down at Shard. "What about him, Brother Werribee?" A plateful awaited Shard, who couldn't eat with his hands tied.

"Act as nanny," Brother Werribee said. "Feed him, right?"

"After I've had mine," Brother Peter said. "I'm ever so hungry, you've no idea. All that way with nothing to eat, it's been *murder*." He sat down, then shot up again, saying "oooh" and clutching his backside. "Who put that there?" His hand came up, holding a small brass door-knob. "Nearly went right up," he said reprovingly.

Brother Werribee gave a coarse laugh. "Never known a poufter complain about that," he said. Brother Peter sat down again in a huff and started on his plateful. When he had finished he came across to Shard and spooned egg and bacon into his mouth, rather messily. "Bloody mother's help now," he said crossly.

"I don't feel like eating anyway," Shard said.

"Oh, it's all right really. After all, you have to eat and you've always spoken to me as though I'm human. Not like some," he added, shooting a malevolent look at Brother Werribee who was munching his way through an extra large portion.

138

Supper out of the way, arrangements were made for the night. Turns would be taken by the brothers and the German to maintain a guard on the prisoner and keep a general watch on the security of the farmhouse in case of intruders, although, as Brother Werribee remarked, there were only bloody sheep to intrude anyway.

Next morning, after the hairstylist had departed, there was a call for Mrs Heffer. The caller was the Home Secretary.

"What is it, Rufus?"

"Candleby, Prime Minister."

"Candleby?" Mrs Heffer sounded blank.

"The – er." You didn't exactly mention the high explosive dump even though there wasn't any secrecy: circumlocutions were second nature to members of the cabinet. "The complaints, Prime – "

"Oh, yes, those *wretched* people in Yorkshire, that's what you mean, isn't it, so why not say so?"

"I'm sorry, Prime Minister – "

"I really *can't think* what they have to complain about, Rufus. To complain is so very unpatriotic I always think. So few people – it's very selfish of them. The stuff has to go somewhere and that part of Yorkshire is *very suitable*."

"I – "

"It's all a great nuisance when I have so many other things to do. And so many worries, Rufus. This Nazi resurgence business being one, as you know very well." Mrs Heffer sighed forbearingly and fluffed critically at her hair. (A shade too stiff? And thinking of shade, was it or was it not time to modify the colour a little? Well, she would have to see.) "I suppose you're trying to rush me into naming a day for our visit, isn't that it, Rufus?"

"Well, Prime Minister, there will be arrangements to be made and so many people to consult, local authorities and so on, and the travel arrangements too – "

"Yes, yes, I'm aware of all that." Mrs Heffer went off at a tangent. "Has anything been heard from the man Sedge? Sedge of the Foreign Office?"

"Rowland Mayes, Prime Minister – "

"You mean you don't know and you're fobbing me off on to the Foreign Secretary. Find out, Rufus, and let me know *immediately*. That's much more important than these wretched people in Yorkshire."

Mrs Heffer put the handset down and frowned at herself in the mirror. As she had said, she detested moaners who put self before country. And she was very surprised that there should be so much fuss. You expected it of Socialists, of course you did, but the rural areas of North Yorkshire had always been Conservative. It was a tradition with the farming community. At least it had been until the Poll Tax. Mrs Heffer gritted her teeth and forced herself not to have more regrets about the Poll Tax. It had crossed her mind to have the high explosives moved to Scotland where again there were more sheep and cows than people; but she understood that there were no natural cave systems in Scotland and the expense of digging out an underground cavern big enough would be simply colossal. There was another consideration too: the only part of Scotland that might, just might, have been to some extent suitable was slap beneath the particular grouse moor that her husband was accustomed to shoot over and she simply could not do that to Percival who was simply splendid and had quite enough to put up with what with her being required by so many people at all hours of the day and night so that they had had scarcely any time alone together for years and years . . . but all the same it was a pity about Scotland because the Scots had so many complaints about everything Conservative under the sun that one more would make no difference to the vote . . .

The telephone rang again.

"Yes. Oh, it's you, Roly."

"Yes, Prime Minister – "

"What about Mr Sedge?"

"Hedge, Prime Minister – "

"Yes, that's what I said. Is there any progress?"

"He's following your orders, Prime Minister – "

"Of course he is. But you haven't answered my question. Has there been any progress?"

"There has been no report as yet – "

"By which you mean there has *not* been any progress. Yes or no, Roly."

"Er – no, Prime – "

The rattle in Rowland Mayes's ear indicated temper on the part of the Prime Minister. Rowland Mayes hissed a little between his teeth but immediately he told himself that that was unfair because Mrs Heffer was such a splendid woman really and of course she was bearing an immense burden, was under immense strain and it was up to her colleagues to make allowances and support her in every way possible. But, since Rowland Mayes had no wish at all to have to report no progress the next time he received a Prime Ministerial prod, he at once telephoned the Knightsbridge number on his security line and got Ms Gunning. It was, he said, time MI5 made an entry to the monastery of God's Anointed. Time, he said, was passing. Ms Gunning agreed that indeed it was and she would pass the message on. Rowland Mayes rang off feeling vaguely put down; Ms Gunning's tone had seemed to convey that he, Her Majesty's Principal Secretary of State for Foreign Affairs, was himself allowing time to pass while he made unnecessary calls to the people who really did the work. Ms Gunning was like that, of course.

"You go in the middle, Brother Ducky. Between Brother Kitchener and Brother Infirmarer. I'll be in the lead with Brother Chamberlain."

"All right," Hedge said, "Reverend Father."

The evacuation was now under way, all the monks in their plain clothes. A lot of weight having been put on in the refectory over the years much of the clothing no longer fitted. They made a motley bunch: tweed jackets like Hedge, jeans, T-shirts, Marks & Spencer's vests in some cases, braces, belts, multi-coloured socks or sandals on bare feet. They followed the route taken by Brothers Werribee and Peter with Shard. There was some difficulty over the replacing behind them of the heavy slab that covered the descent shaft. Brother Chamberlain, the ex chucker-out, shifting his place in the line, said that he could manage where lesser men would fail. Going down last, he hefted the slab, with much swearing, as close to the hole as he could whilst leaving enough room to admit his own body, and then, with his feet anchored firmly on the ladder, he reached back up and inched the slab into position, lifting it just clear of the ground with his tremendous strength until it dropped with a muted thud into place. The job completed, Hedge heard him remark somewhat loudly that he had bloody near given himself a fucking hernia.

Hedge himself had difficulty later on with the path alongside the underground waterfall, which crashed and thundered alarmingly in his ears. In the end, after much bad-tempered argument and references to Brother Ducky being aptly named, Hedge was carried bodily by Brother Chamberlain and Brother Infirmarer between them. The rest of the way was uneventful; and they emerged from the exit into the darkness of night and into a very cold wind with more than a hint of rain to come. Salisbury Plain stood bare and grim and empty. Empty, that was except for one gloomy, anoraked man who approached Reverend Father and said everything was tickety-boo and would the brothers all follow him, please.

They did, in single file, Hedge once again between Brother Kitchener and Brother Infirmarer. They followed down to a road, a side road that was really little more, in fact, than a tank track that led to another road where two coaches were waiting. When all had piled aboard, the coaches headed for a bigger road, the main road, Reverend Father said, that ran from Salisbury north to Swindon.

Hedge asked where they were going.

Reverend Father said, "Have a guess, Brother Ducky."

Hedge thought. "Yorkshire?" he said.

"Top of the class," Reverend Father said, grinning.

Well, it was obvious really, Hedge thought, since Candleby in the Pennines was to be the scene of the big explosion. Hedge was by now frantic with worry: he really should be escaping, taking the terrible news to London, or anyway phoning it through, before Mrs Heffer went north. He really must not fail her; if he did, well, of course she would no longer be there to reprove him for throwing her trust back in her face, but his name would still be mud. If he himself survived, that was, which he might not. He had a sudden vision, a stupid but blinding one, of himself and Mrs Heffer travelling into the sky together, her voice angrily upbraiding him for his utter incompetence and telling him that on no account would God ever forgive him because once they reached His presence she would tell Him the full story of how he, was it Hedge or Sedge, had been the instrument that had left Great Britain bereft of strong leadership . . .

Next morning, with a watery look in the sky over the farmhouse, the telephone rang again and Brother Werribee answered. He spoke in monosyllables, then imparted news.

"Harry," he said. "They've made it to Fountains. We link up this evening, nine p.m. At Jervaulx, not Fountains. After that, Reverend Father will tell us the next move, right?"

Klaus and Brother Peter nodded. Brother Werribee looked down at Shard. "You'll be sorted out, I reckon, at Jervaulx." He gave a coarse laugh. "Tell you something, shall I?"

"Go ahead."

"Word of advice: prepare to meet thy God. Reverend Father'll likely shove you down the big hole so you go with the bang, right?"

There was an immediate reaction from Klaus The Long Knife: the German hadn't liked the mention of the hole or the bang and was signalling his dislike with his eyes. Brother Werribee said carelessly, "So what the hell! He's not going to get away."

Shard, not going to get away, thought he might get an answer to a question in the circumstances. Or might not; the look in The Long Knife's eyes was against it. Brother Werribee wouldn't be risking any further leaks: the German was known to be a dangerous man.

Fountains was very bleak. The air was damp and as at the exit from the fissure on to Salisbury Plain, now well south, the wind was blowing. The custodian at the entry was concealed in his little wooden hut, but ready to pounce out to take the money for the car park. The coaches halted; Reverend Father leaned down. His hand held a number of five pound notes.

"Private party," he said.

The custodian looked into the leading coach. "Any OAPs, are there? Any National Trust members?"

"No OAPs. No National Trust members. We're a party of social workers. On a course," Reverend Father added. "Field training."

"*Field* training?" The custodian seemed astonished.

"The *social* field, my dear fellow, not the agricultural one," Reverend Father said. "Investigating the vagaries of human nature and all that." Cousin Wally, Hedge thought sourly, was managing to look quite like a social worker: he wore an open-necked shirt, grubby jeans, and wore one earring plus a thin gold chain round his neck.

"Not from these parts?" the custodian asked.

"No, no. Cambridge." The coaches bore the name of a firm in Ely. The custodian waved them through and they ground on into the car park, scattering the perennial ducks, Hedge hoping there would be no jokes on his adopted name. They disembarked and set off in double file for the Valley of the Seven Bridges. Hedge caused a diversion. "I need to go to the lavatory," he said to Brother Infirmarer. He had noted a sign to the Ladies and Gents at the far end of the car park, a rather muddy end. Hedge's need was genuine enough but there was an ulterior motive: a hope, however forlorn it might be, that there could be an avenue of escape.

But not so. "Pee from one of the bridges," Brother Kitchener said, "or along the track if it's that urgent."

It was urgent and not only in the case of Hedge. But it was all right: it was early and there were only the resident cows to watch. The calls of nature answered, the supposed social workers plodded on across the bridges, entered the heavily wooded area at the end of the dale or valley, found the rocky overhang and the beck where they were met by the ferocious-looking skinhead who announced that he would guide them the rest of the way and that Arry from Ripon was inside.

"Inside?"

144

"Not in that sense. Inside the bloody rock. Reverend Father," the skinhead added as an afterthought, remembering Arry had said this bloke was particular. They all followed him in, along the beck and the underground passage, through the hole and into the compartment where the high explosives were stacked. Hedge gave a shiver; he was now, he supposed, in the very bowels of the earth where the explosion was to take place. There would be absolutely no chance now of escape. No chance to issue a warning, though by now such consideration had taken a poor second place to anxieties about his own skin. He uttered a sharp cry of alarm when, alongside him, Brother Kitchener stumbled over a small projection of rock.

"Bugger," said Brother Kitchener, rubbing his shinbone.

"Is . . . is this the place?" Hedge asked, his mouth dry with terror and his flesh crawling.

"Only a part of it." It was Reverend Father who answered. "Just a small offshoot. All the same, there's quite enough here, Brother Ducky, to despatch you to Kingdom Come."

"You too," Hedge said through set teeth.

"Oh, yes. But naturally I'll not be here when the time comes, will I?"

"And – and me? Do you mean – "

"That depends, Brother Ducky," Reverend Father said. "You see, dear cousin, we have a use for you. You are to be the magnet, don't you see? Or shall we say the fuse?"

Hedge felt the last of his courage drain away. The magnet . . . magnets and explosives, they could perhaps go together in some dreadful way. The fuse . . . there could be some as yet unimagined horror in which his body could be used as it were to touch the match to the flintlock or whatever. "Magnet?" he managed to ask.

"The magnet that draws the brass to Candleby. The brass, with Mrs Heffer, dear boy."

"H-h-how?"

"You'll be given full details later," Reverend Father assured him. After that he would say no more. Hedge, as the party advanced behind the beam of the torch carried by the skinhead, felt his stomach loosen. He was absolutely done

145

for; the one slight ray of hope lay in the fact, the possible fact anyway, that by now Whitehall as represented by the Head of Security upon whose orders he was acting might be concerned about him, he not having been in touch since his departure on his supposed defection. The authorities might be worried; Mrs Heffer included. And surely, if she was worried, she would do something about him, put the wheels of succour in motion? But she would have to hurry before she, too, was blown into little pieces.

Later that day, with the man called Arry now leading, there was a mass exodus. The exodus took place along a fissure in the rock that led off from the cavern into a blankness that brought more terror to Hedge as he stumbled along between Brothers Kitchener and Infirmarer. He knew not where they were going other than yet deeper and deeper into the bowels of the earth. Earlier conversation between Arry and Reverend Father had told Hedge just one thing: they were about to join up with the advance party that had left Stockbridge by tunnel prior to Hedge's arrival there, and the advance party would, Hedge was now certain, include Shard. And a fat lot of use Shard had turned out to be − a closely-guarded prisoner like himself. There were many things Hedge could say to Shard when they met but he was already too dispirited to say them. No doubt a dignified, forbearing silence would be the best way. One more point of hope had occurred to Hedge earlier and he still clung to that hope even though Reverend Father had dashed it on enquiry. MI5 would surely by this time have descended in force upon the monastery of God's Anointed and would have probed deeply.

Reverend Father had shrugged that off with a laugh. "They'll find nothing of any help at all," he said. "That's been seen to, Brother Ducky."

"But suppose they find that slab, and the descent?"

"Oh, they probably will."

"So if they do − "

"It really won't matter, dear boy. It simply ends on Salisbury Plain, doesn't it? No clues from there. Just a nice blank."

Yes, that was true. Hedge said, "But surely . . . all this is terribly unwieldy, isn't it?" As a defector who was there to help, it was imperative he should take an interest. "I mean – "

"If it's unwieldy for us, it's unwieldy for the government, isn't it?"

"Oh," Hedge considered this point. "What you're saying is, if you don't know what you're doing, neither do they?"

Reverend Father had laughed and clapped his hands. "Oh, well put indeed, Brother Ducky . . . only it's inaccurate as it happens. I know very, very well what I'm doing, don't worry."

Hedge had thereafter remained silent. Yet, as the awful underground journey continued, seemingly without end, he was still able to nurture his hope. Even MI5 couldn't possibly be so stupid as to find nothing of consequence in the monastery, nor so stupid as to deduce nothing from the admitted blankness of Salisbury Plain at the tunnel's end.

Or could they?

Soon Hedge was forced to proceed on hands and knees as the headroom came sharply down. He kept on butting his head into the buttocks of Brother Infirmarer who after the sixth butt protested angrily that he wasn't bloody Brother Peter and would Brother Ducky please leave his bloody bum alone or when they reached journey's end he would give him what for.

Hedge apologised but when he tried to hang back he got further complaints from Brother Kitchener, this time about his feet.

THIRTEEN

Hedge was most terribly tired long before journey's end was reached, journey's end being beneath the ruins of Jervaulx Abbey, a distance of perhaps around fifteen miles, or less by fissure, and which felt a lot longer even though they had rested half way in a part where the fissure widened out into a sort of chamber. Reverend Father had remarked that they were not far from Mother Shipton's cave, the place where Mother Shipton, or her present-day representative, accepted for a fee articles from tourists for fossilisation and collection around six months later, there being some very special property about the air or water or something in the cave. Mother Shipton's, Hedge happened to know, was not far from the large city of Harrogate, between there and Ripon, quite a populous area beneath which to site an enormous and dangerous explosives store; and he remarked on this during the stand easy.

"Oh, there are no explosives here, Brother Ducky. They're behind us and to the east and north."

"I thought you said the dump at Fountains was only a part?"

"Yes, indeed I did. But only a very small part and none of the storehouse system leads this way. It extends by way of other fissures such as this one . . . north and east, a long way, dear boy, until it terminates beneath Cam Fell and Foxup Moor . . . between Langstrothdale Chase and Horton-in-Ribblesdale. Potholing country – Candleby. But of course all the entries to the magazine itself are very effectively sealed off, with no chance of anyone getting in."

"Then how do you – "

"I should have said, no chance of anyone getting in *by accident*."

Hedge nodded; Cousin Wally would of course have his entry nicely prepared. Hedge had heard from Whitehall sources that the underground complex was unguarded. No need had ever been seen to put the system under guard, but Hedge believed that there was a remote control surveillance in existence, something to do with electronics or television or maybe computers. When he mentioned this to Reverend Father in the hopes of deflecting him from his purpose, it turned out that he knew the facts already. Hedge wondered about the explosives near Fountains Abbey, a long way from Cam Fell and Candleby, and the very open entry to the cavern where they lay. He asked Reverend Father about this.

Reverend Father said, "They've only recently arrived there, dear boy."

"Oh."

"By arrangements of my own. This is currently unknown to your mandarins in Whitehall. And I have my own guards, who are well able to deflect the odd potholer."

Hedge saw the point: one look at the skinhead would be enough for anybody, and no doubt there would be other skinheads to share his duties. Reverend Father went on, "I need hardly tell you, I do not propose to be anywhere near Foxup Moor when the whole shebang goes up. Hence my little store at Fountains. I'm sure you've heard of fuse trails, dear boy. I have any number of reels of fuse wire. And there's a trail already in position."

"All the way along?"

"All the way along, Brother Ducky, all the way along."

Hedge's brain whirled: Cousin Wally, by the sound of it, couldn't fail. Mrs Heffer, also many innocent farmers and other inhabitants of the area – probably all the people in Horton-in-Ribblesdale – were now in immense danger of their lives. Hedge very nearly fainted with the awful burden of his knowledge: he really ought to make a bid for escape, but where was the chance of that now? It was obviously non-existent. And he remembered all those weapons in Cousin Wally's apparently private cave. Probably they were there for eventual use by Klaus The Long Knife, who would perhaps go into action when that bastion of liberty (Mrs Heffer) had been blown into little fragments . . .

Soon after this the party was got on the move again. When finally they stopped Hedge, who was almost out on his feet, flopped to the ground more dead than alive. His sleep verged on unconsciousness; it was impossible to rouse him, even though Brother Werribee, who had now joined the main party along with Shard and Brother Peter and the German, tried to do so with a kick in the ribs. In this almost drugged sleep Hedge suffered alarming hallucinations and terrifying dreams. In one nightmare he was back at Stockbridge and had under pressure attended Compline. The monks taunted him, laughing at his tonsure and the way he wore his unaccustomed habit, and then they had all pelted him with paper darts made from prayer sheets. Another dream concerned Mrs Heffer. Mrs Heffer was with the Queen, insisting that it was necessary to have a royal presence at the explosives dump, and Her Majesty had bravely offered herself but her offer had been sunk without trace by the Lord Privy Seal who had reminded Mrs Heffer that the presence of Her Majesty would be bound to steal her own thunder, whereupon Mrs Heffer had rounded on the Queen and had accused her of interfering in matters that were the sole concern of a duly elected parliament and Britain was, after all, a democracy . . . A very disturbing element in the dream was that the Lord Privy Seal had actually appeared as a seal, shiny and with flippers and whiskers and a friendly face topped by a gold coronet. It was at this point that another kick, a heavy one, was aimed at Hedge and he woke to find the seal's friendly face merging into the truculent one of Brother Werribee.

"All bloody poms do is bloody sleep," the Australian brother said. "You're wanted, Brother Ducky. Reverend Father."

Hedge struggled from sleep. "W-what for?" he asked.

"Make a bloody phone call."

"No, Rufus, Tuesday will *not* suit. I have a delegation from the Women's Institutes as you should very well know."

"Yes, Prime Minister, but this inspection is becoming a most important matter – "

"So is the women's vote."

"Undoubtedly, Prime Minister. But a postponement will not, I feel sure, have any long term effect on the women's vote, whereas the farmers – "

"*Tuesday will not suit.* Is that clear, Rufus?"

The Home Secretary gave a sigh. "Yes, Prime Minister." When he had withdrawn, Mrs Heffer got to her feet and went across to a window from which she could catch a glimpse of Whitehall at the end of Downing Street. All those people, hurrying about their business or going to and coming from the Jobcentres ... Conservatives, Socialists, various kinds of Liberals, Greens and other fringe groups including the Monster Raving Loonies or whatever. Such a variety; but most of those people, she believed, were Conservatives at heart even if on occasions they were stupid enough to vote Labour. A kind of mental aberration, really, for which they couldn't perhaps be blamed, a sort of involuntary mad cow disease induced by clever – yes, she would admit a degree of cleverness – Labour propaganda. Such a *useless* bunch ... Mrs Heffer steeled herself. As Prime Minister of Great Britain, she was the leader of them all and never mind their political persuasions. She must act in the best interests of the whole country and hope that when election time came they would all see sense and become, once again, True Blue. Blue was such a *positive* colour, which green and yellow and rose pink were not and never would be. She alone stood guard between the largely unthinking masses (Socialists, that was) and the horrid threat of the mailed fist of a resurgent and re-unified Germany as represented by this madman they called Klaus The Long Knife, such a stupid thing to be called when you really thought about it – all this, and Rufus could think of nothing but the wretched farming communities in North Yorkshire and their sheep. Although Mrs Heffer well recognised that her presence alone would give an immense uplift to the Yorkshire people's morale, there were currently much more important considerations – and where, for heaven's sake, was Mr Sedge?

Hedge was walking along a road, the road that led past Jervaulx Abbey's ruins from Ripon to Leyburn on the fringe of Wensleydale. With him, close on either side, were Brothers Werribee and Infirmarer; the strong arms of Brother Chamberlain (arms that would have made a more effective escort than those of Brother Infirmarer, a skinny man who before entering the monastery had been a failed male nurse) being otherwise occupied in mounting guard on Shard back in the fissure, which had in fact come to an end beneath a concealing heap of stones in the abbey's ruins.

In the small village of East Witton stood a telephone box. Hedge was led towards this. While the escorting brothers lounged outside Hedge entered the box with Reverend Father, who was also accompanying the party.

Money – pound coins, fifty-pence pieces and an array of smaller stuff – was thrust into Hedge's hand. "You know what to say," Reverend Father said.

"Yes."

"Don't make a cock of it, then."

To his immense alarm, Hedge felt the hard snout of an automatic against his spine. Cousin Wally was turning nasty, showing his true colours and his basic lack of trust in his kinsman.

Hedge pressed the buttons for Downing Street.

"I wish to speak to the Prime Minister," he said in a high, unnatural voice. "My name is Hedge and the matter is most urgent."

Brother Chamberlain had absented himself. "Gone for a pee," Brother Peter said informatively.

"Where?" Shard asked.

Brother Peter jerked a thumb upwards. "Open air. In the ruins."

"Won't he be seen?"

"If he is, he's just a tourist. No-one'll ask questions."

152

"I see. How long do we stay here, Brother Peter?"

"Don't know, do I? Up to Reverend Father, that is." Brother Peter added, "P'raps we'll know more when Reverend Father gets back with your mate."

Shard nodded. It was now known that he and Hedge were connected professionally: Hedge's reaction when coming out of his trance-like sleep had been lacking in circumspection. He had addressed Shard by name in the hearing of Reverend Father and the cat had leapt finally out of the bag, confirming Reverend Father's earlier guess back in the monastery. The only difference it had made had been that henceforward Shard was more closely guarded. He was not questioned again; now his boss was here, it would be the boss who would get the questions, and Reverend Father himself was in personal charge in that respect. In the meantime Shard was keeping his eyes and ears open and he had already heard quite a lot. He knew broadly what was going to happen; his own concern was to get away from custody and crack the threat wide open before the Abbot of Stockbridge went into action.

Which was easier said than done.

Brother Chamberlain came back from his errand. "Nobody up there," he said. "Quiet as a bleeding nunnery." He laughed; it had been a joke. Brother Peter laughed too, sycophantically, and wriggled his bottom. Brother Chamberlain contemplated the wriggle and said, "Don't you go giving me ideas, you little pouf."

"Oooh, I never!" Brother Peter flounced away, making towards the exit to the open air above.

"Mr Sedge, how are you? And *where* are you? And what is going on? Why are you and not the Foreign Secretary ringing me?"

"Prime Minister – "

"Yes, it is I. What have you to tell me, Mr Sedge?"

"Prime Minister, I'm currently unable to tell you where I am or indeed very much else. I don't know if you understand."

"I don't believe I do, Mr Sedge. Perhaps you can explain."

"I can't do that either," Hedge said desperately. "Not fully that is. I am – er."

"You are what?" Mrs Heffer shook the telephone; it was probably a bad line, so typical of British Telecom, she would speak to someone about it. "What did you say, Mr Sedge?"

There was a pause, quite a long one, and clicks and clanks as more money was fed into the system. Hedge, though this Mrs Heffer was not to know, was in conference with Reverend Father. Hedge was asking what he was to say, having forgotten his precise orders under the battering of Mrs Heffer's inquisition. Reverend Father hissed, "Tell the old trout you're under duress, but don't give away any clues."

"Yes," Hedge said, and Reverend Father took his hand away from the mouthpiece. Hedge, once again in communication, said, "I'm under duress, Prime Minister."

"Under *what*?"

Hedge shouted, "Duress."

There was an indistinct sound, one of horror, incredulity and great anger. "Do you mean you've been *captured*, Mr Sedge?"

Hedge said, "Yes, Prime Minister."

"How *absolutely monstrous*. I've never heard of such a thing, I must say, an official of the Foreign Office . . . who by?"

"The neo-Nazis, Prime Minister. The German – "

"Those people." There was immense contempt in Mrs Heffer's voice. She said scornfully, "Fancy letting such *wicked* people get their hands on you! I suppose you were overpowered, though."

"Yes, Prime Minister."

"How very terrible. Now, tell me if you can why you're ringing me, Mr Sedge. Are your captors present?"

Yes, Hedge said, they were. He had a message for her and he must pass it quickly before his change ran out and because of other considerations, by which he meant before a tap could be put on the line, or rather (since Whitehall lines were always tapped) before the call box could be located. And he urged her to listen very carefully indeed to his message and to be sure to act upon it because his captors meant every word they said. Hedge was so terrified that he sounded very con-

154

vincing indeed. And afterwards Reverend Father seemed quite satisfied.

After a preliminary telephone call to the Home Secretary, Mrs Heffer called an emergency meeting of her cabinet.

"A call from your Mr Sedge, Roly. He was in distress. Such a very brave man ... he was overpowered by these *wicked* men after putting up a staunch resistance, I expect. One would expect no less, of course. We're all British, as I told the Queen only recently and she agreed." Mrs Heffer paused. "Mr Sedge had a message. A message from these *desperadoes*. The message was quite simple. It concerns the aspirations of the desperadoes. As we have already suspected, of course, their aim, their ultimate intention, is to take over the government of this country, the *duly elected* government of this country of ours."

"A *coup d'état*, Prime Minister?"

"No, Roly, not a *coup d'état*. Only *foreigners* have *coups d'état*. South Americans and so on. I prefer to call it a dastardly and cowardly attempt to seduce our people from their loyalties. And," Mrs Heffer added vehemently, throwing out her breasts, "they'll not succeed."

There was a chorus of of course nots, who do they think they are. Mrs Heffer nodded vigorously throughout this response. It was the Secretary of State for Defence who put the sixty-four thousand dollar question: "What is the nature of the threat, Prime Minister?"

"I've already told you that," Mrs Heffer said coldly.

"I beg your pardon, Prime Minister. I'll put it a different way. What is the threatened alternative, if their demands are not met ... by which I take it they're demanding that you step down? Without bloodshed."

"That is exactly what poor Mr Sedge said. And of course I shall never step down as you put it, Defence Secretary. And, as I said, as Mr Sedge put it. They ought to know me better than *that* I would have thought."

The Defence Secretary gave a discreet cough. "Prime Minister, what I'm anxious to elucidate is this: what if you don't stand down? What do they do then?"

155

"I was coming to that," Mrs Heffer stated. "It all has to do with that explosives dump up in Yorkshire. The one that's been in the news recently because of the fuss made by the farming people, the sheep and so on," she said, giving the impression that the livestock had themselves joined in the row.

Rowland Mayes, his face pale, asked, "Are they threatening to blow it up, Prime Minister? Is that the alternative? Because if so, then a very considerable amount of destruction will be caused, and a lot of casualties, and I . . . " His voice tailed away under the sheer violence of Mrs Heffer's look in his direction.

"What pusillanimity, Foreign Secretary! Naturally, I would be the *first* to deplore any casualties among our people, but really! One does not collapse at the first fence, Foreign Secretary. As I've said before, we're British and like poor, brave Mr Sedge it's up to us, to me anyway, to stick it out and fight back in defence of the realm. We are a proud people, Foreign Secretary, and we never surrender. I believe Mr Churchill said that once and he was right."

"Yes indeed, Prime Minister." Rowland Mayes, acting bravely himself, pressed his point. "But are we in fact to take it that an explosion really is on the cards?"

"Yes," Mrs Heffer said. "That is precisely the case. And now, I suppose, somebody is going to suggest an evacuation of the area. I forbid any such thing – there will *be no evacuation*. The reason being that Mr Sedge made it quite clear that at the very first sign of an evacuation, or indeed of any other precautions such as the movement of troops or police, the whole area will be *immediately* blown up."

"But only if you refuse to accede. Refuse to stand down." This was the Home Secretary, who spoke in the flat tones of defeat, Mrs Heffer having already said she would never surrender. She said it again.

"Exactly, Home Secretary. And stand down I shall not. The people trust me. There is, however, what one might call, I suppose, an escape clause." She paused, jaw set and eyes flashing her determination. "It is one I propose to take advantage of."

156

There was an air of expectancy, also of relief. An escape clause was good news and it might get the cabinet off the hook of having to make a decision or even, which God forbid, the worse hook of having perhaps to oppose Mrs Heffer. They all waited with bated breath.

Mrs Heffer said, "Mr Sedge was precise and left me in *no doubt* that these people mean what they say." There was another pause. "Mr Sedge spoke of the forthcoming visit we're to make to the threatened area. To reassure the farming communities. That is known to the desperadoes, you see. And it is to take place tomorrow."

The Home Secretary gave an apologetic little cough. "Tomorrow is Tuesday, Prime Minister – "

"Yes, I know that, thank you, Rufus."

"The Women's Institute, Prime Minister – "

"Not the Women's Institute, the Townswomen's Guild I believe – "

"But surely – "

"Kindly don't interrupt me, Home Secretary, and whoever they are, they'll have to wait. The security of our country comes first and I shouldn't have to remind you of that. In any case we must go along with Mr Sedge who is the man on the spot. And he stipulates tomorrow. There is to be what Mr Sedge speaks of as a parley. That is what I regard as an escape clause."

No-one else did. "A parley with the desperadoes, Prime Minister?"

"Yes. Naturally, I shall concede nothing. But nothing will be lost by talking to the ringleader. So we shall go. Rufus, you shall make the arrangements. And remember, there are to be *no special precautions* – I've already explained that."

"Yes, Prime Minister. But is there not an element of extreme danger? To the persons including yourself – "

"No, Rufus, I rather think not. If there had been, I'm quite sure Mr Sedge would have found a way of putting the information across. And I believe that it will be seen to be *my presence* that will prove the guarantee of safety for us all. These vile persons would never, quite obviously, take the risk of injuring me. They are well aware of the *esteem* . . . they

157

would never risk alienating our people, never risk jeopardising their plans in advance. I should have thought that would be obvious. And in any case, I at any rate will not be put off by thoughts of danger."

There was nothing further to be said. Firmly, Mrs Heffer brought the cabinet meeting to a closure and walked out of the room with her head high. She left dismay and disbelief in her wake. The Defence Secretary was heard to mutter that it was a very curious escape clause, one that appeared to offer no escape at all in fact. When the parley ended as it would in vehement rejection from Mrs Heffer, the desperadoes would go into action. Another minister was heard to say that the desperadoes obviously had Mrs Heffer weighed off to a t. "Too bloody obstinate to resist a challenge of that sort," he said. "And that being so . . . God help us all."

FOURTEEN

The next move was made by coach; the one belonging to the firm in Ely that had brought the main party from Stockbridge to Fountains Abbey. In the early morning of Tuesday this coach parked in the car park opposite the gate into the grounds of Jervaulx, parking close to a peacock that seemed not to mind the intrusion. The driver walked across the Ripon to Leyburn road and entered the grounds of the ruined abbey. Once inside the second gate, the one where the honest paid their entry fee into the waiting box, he gave a whistle. As if from nowhere Brother Peter appeared.

"Oooh, it's you. Isn't it ever such a lovely day?"

"Right, it is. Where's Reverend Father?"

"In the ablutions."

"Ablutions?"

"Behind the hedge."

"Oh, ah." At that moment Reverend Father appeared from behind a large bush, zipping up his fly. "Good man," he called to the coach driver. "No problems?"

"None at all, Reverend Father. Everything's set. Should be where you want by eight-thirty latest, all right?"

"Yes," Reverend Father said, and vanished as suddenly as Brother Peter had appeared. Brother Peter followed after and the driver ambled back to his coach, where the peacock had been joined by his mate and half-a-dozen hens. In the fissure beneath the ruins the monks made ready for departure under the general direction of Brother Werribee who was something of a regimental sergeant-major.

"Get a bloody move on, right? Shower of useless bastards," he remarked to Shard as he squatted alongside and untied Shard's wrists and ankles. "Don't let freedom go to your head, cobber. It's just because we don't want to attract any attention . . . I'll be right behind you with a gun. Or someone will. So don't try anything we don't like."

"Where are we going?"

The answer was the standard one: "You'll see."

Brother Werribee went away and his place was taken by Brother Peter, who repeated the warning about not trying anything funny. "Only rub off on me," he said rather pathetically. "I'm the one what always gets the bloody blame, specially from that blooming Brother Werribee. He's such a bully and me, I'm all for peace and quiet."

"Like an explosion?"

Brother Peter wriggled in what looked like embarrassment. "Don't blame me. I got let in for this lot. I didn't want to, honest I didn't."

"Peace and love," Shard murmured, flexing wrists and ankles, getting the blood flowing again. "And it's nice, isn't it, to be back in Yorkshire again?"

Brother Peter nodded vigorously. "Oh yes, that's ever so nice."

"Home territory, Brother Peter. Worth thinking about, isn't it?"

Brother Peter looked at him suspiciously. "Not suggesting anything, are you?"

"Yes, I am."

"Oh." Brother Peter looked a little disconcerted. "What?"

"What I've suggested before. Get out from under, the first chance you get. You've never been happy in the monastery, you know that."

"No. It's not really me, that I will say . . . all them prayers and bloody Brother Werribee, it's been a right pain it has and if I'd never bloody gone into the Triar Fuck, beg pardon, the Friar Tuck – you know, the caff in Amesbury, I told you – "

"Yes, you did, Brother Peter. So take that first chance. You don't want to risk being blown up, do you?"

"Well, no. No, I don't." Brother Peter sat on the ground of

160

the cave and looked very thoughtful. "I don't suppose you do either."

"No. So if it's any help, I'll come with you."

"With me?"

Shard said, "When you scarper, Brother Peter."

"Would you really?"

"If you insist," Shard said gravely.

"Oooh, you're having me on, you know you are. Reverend Father'd never let you go."

Tuesday – this very day – having once been rejected in favour of Mrs Heffer's other engagement, there was now a considerable degree of last-minute panic among the local authority and the police. It was all very well that Mrs Heffer had ordered no extra precautions: she would nevertheless expect the minimum of dignity to be attendant upon her visit and with Mrs Heffer minimum dignity and deference was a pretty large undertaking. Her car would of course require a police escort with outriders, there was nothing 'extra' about that. The Lord Lieutenant of the county of North Yorkshire was at first briefed (mistakenly) to be there in his uniform, plus the chairman of the Rural District Council and various sheriffs and so on together with their acolytes and of course the National Farmers' Union, local branch, would be there in force to put their views to the Prime Minister, none of them, naturally, knowing that at any moment their cause and their land as well might go sky high, taking themselves along with it. No word of the threat had been released by Downing Street and therefore everything was to be beautifully laid on including a big luncheon in a vast marquee to be erected on some more or less flat ground near the Ribblehead viaduct that carried the Skipton to Carlisle railway on its scenic journey through the fells and dales.

At the last moment there had come a decree from Durham that the bishop intended to be present so that he could put certain points about the wickedness of armaments to Mrs Heffer in person. With him would come the Dean and those members of the chapter that were not required for duty elsewhere or who were not on holiday. This complicated the

161

seating arrangements for the luncheon in the marquee and books of reference giving the Order of Precedence were hurriedly consulted. It was later intimated that no royalty would be present and this intimation caused the Lord Lieutenant to indicate that his presence would be superfluous and indeed unconstitutional. However, as a special mark of respect to Mrs Heffer, who was known to appreciate such gestures, the Lord Lieutenant was prevailed upon to attend though not, after all, in uniform. This was seen as a fair and reasonable compromise.

Mrs Heffer and her entourage would leave King's Cross by train for York, and at York railway station she would be met by a red carpet, the Lord Mayor, and a limousine to carry her into the northern dales. The luncheon would in fact, on account of the time factor, be held before, not after, the tour of inspection and the confab with the farmers' union. And (although this was known only to the cabinet) before the parley with the desperadoes.

"Mr Sedge," Mrs Heffer said before leaving Downing Street at an unaccustomedly early hour, "said nothing about *how* these persons are to make contact with me. His telephone call was a hurried one and of course I was unable to call him back. What do you think, Roly?"

"About what, Prime Minister?"

"Oh, about *how they'll make contact*, of course!"

"Well, Prime Minister." Rowland Mayes, never at his best in the early morning, thought hard as to how he was to answer an unanswerable question. "It's hard to say. With foreigners, you – "

"Of course they're foreigners. It's *because* they're foreigners," Mrs Heffer said snappishly, "that I asked you the question. You're supposed to be my Foreign Secretary."

"Yes, Prime Minister. Well, it's very hard to say. A direct approach . . . "

"Or an indirect one?"

"Precisely, Prime Minister."

Mrs Heffer gave a snorting sound and turned her back on him. Rowland Mayes wriggled in forlorn embarrassment; he

162

had always tried to do his very best and it wasn't always appreciated. Mrs Heffer thereafter addressed the Home Secretary. "Let us hope," she said, "that it's not done too *publicly*. Well, are we all ready?"

The expected chorus came on cue. "Yes, Prime Minister."

Mrs Heffer led the way into the street and the car, saluted on her way into danger and perhaps glory by the policeman on guard duty. It was sheerly coincidental that as she stepped into the car the sound of heavy gunfire came from the direction of the Tower of London where the King's Troop of the Royal Horse Artillery were rehearsing for Her Majesty's birthday.

Before the desperadoes left the cave beneath Jervaulx' ruins Klaus The Long Knife passed his final orders to Cousin Wally and the brothers.

"It is of course I who shall conduct the parley. How, where and when, this is not yet possible to decide. I shall play it, as you would say, by ear. We do not know the arrangements for the visit of the Heffer. But broadly the plan is so simple. Is this not so, Brother Werribee?"

"So long as the bloody motor-bike's ready and working," Brother Werribee said. His orders were that on arrival at a certain spot off the Horton-in-Ribblesdale road he was to leave the coach party accompanied by a radio transceiver, take over a motor cycle that would be waiting, having been ridden there by the man Arry from Ripon, and ride fast for the Fountains cavern beyond the Valley of the Seven Bridges. Here he would stand by for orders, if they came which he believed they would, to start the fuse trail that would sputter its way underground towards the great explosives dump beneath Langstrothdale Chase. The order to do so would come by means of three long dashes and two short dots of the Morse Code on a radio supplied and operated by Brother Chamberlain. After this Brother Werribee would make himself scarce together with the guarding skinhead. Back in the vicinity of Langstrothdale Chase, The Long Knife's supporters would then have some forty-five minutes to belt like bats out of hell from the danger area. Klaus's plan, exact

163

timing yet to be decided, was to appear for the parley before the Prime Minister began her tour of inspection to prove to the Yorkshire farmers that the dump was perfectly safe and they had nothing to worry about. If the parley should fail on account of Mrs Heffer's obduracy, then Klaus would hold his hand, and Brother Chamberlain would hold his radio, until Mrs Heffer and the brass had vanished into the bowels of the earth below Langstrothdale Chase and Cam Fell. After that, the set events would follow as the night the day and Klaus, with the assistance of Hedge's Cousin Wally, would activate his waiting contacts and begin the process of taking over control of the central government in the midst of the cataclysm that would follow the devastation of a huge area of North Yorkshire and the fragmentation of the Prime Minister, a number of her senior colleagues, the Chief of the General Staff, sundry sheriffs and (as an additional bonus as yet unknown to the conspirators) the Lord Bishop of Durham.

The resumé concluded, the brothers began to emerge from the earth beneath the ruins and to stream, looking just like any ordinary band of tourists from a coach in their jeans and T-shirts and anoraks, out of the gate, across the field and then the road, to embark aboard the coach from Ely. Shard, with Brother Peter's gun in his back, contrived to come up alongside Hedge, who was being trusted enough in his capacity as Reverend Father's cousin not to need an escort. Hedge whispered, "Shard, for heaven's sake don't come too close."

"Why not?"

"It'll look as though we're in cahoots."

"And aren't we, Hedge?"

"Yes. No. Oh, I suppose so. But I really don't know."

"Whose side are you on, Hedge?"

Hedge said frigidly, "Matters are very difficult between me and my – er – second cousin. Touchy. I have to be very careful, don't you see?"

"And Mrs Heffer?"

"Oh, don't remind me!" Hedge was in a bad state of nerves. "I do know she can't possibly be allowed to blow up. It's all

164

very unfortunate and such a worry. I really don't know what to do."

Shard said cynically as he negotiated a cowpat, "Nothing you can do, is there?"

"Well – no."

"Except escape. And then tell all."

"Escape?" Hedge went pale. "Oh, that would just be to – to court disaster. Wouldn't it?"

"Think of Mrs Heffer, Hedge."

"Oh, I have been, constantly. Constantly."

"Then do your duty and act for her. We have help at hand, Hedge. Brother Peter. He's with us. I think. Just so long as Brother Werribee doesn't get to hear too soon."

"Oh, dear. What are you suggesting, Shard?"

"That we grab Brother Peter's gun, or he hands it over. Not here – in the coach. Then we can nab the lot, with luck. A clean sweep, Hedge, before the point of no return. Just think about it. Think of the honour, Hedge. Think of saving Mrs Heffer's life."

"Yes, there is that. Yes. I'll think about it, Shard."

"So having thought, Hedge, just be ready when I give the word. And now shut up. Brother Werribee's coming back along the line."

There was a sound of fright from behind and the gun dug harder into Shard's back. Hedge scuttled ahead towards Cousin Wally. Shard sent up a prayer that Brother Peter wouldn't weaken. Brother Werribee reached them with remarks about tail-end Charlies, little poufters who couldn't keep up with the rest. They all moved on for the car park, where the sudden rush at last disturbed the peacock who departed screeching with his attendant hens. With all checked aboard by Brother Werribee the coach drove out of the car park and headed towards Middleham and the village of Wensley at the head of the dale, Cousin Wally sitting in the front like a headmaster in charge of a school treat, with Hedge next to him. Hedge was pondering Shard's final remark: "So having thought, Hedge, just be ready when I give the word." The phrasing meant undoubtedly that Shard had already decided his thinking for him and was taking it for

165

granted that he would give his support.

But how could he, sitting right next to Reverend Father and a long way, as coach interiors went, from Shard and Brother Peter?

"How kind of you to meet me, my Lord Mayor." Mrs Heffer was as ever gracious. She had set foot on the red carpet followed by Rowland Mayes and the Home Secretary and the rest, including the CGS and some other uniformed brass from the Defence Ministry, chair-seat polishers, plus a vice-admiral who had come up from Devonport as a pier-head jump to represent naval interests, there being some submarine missile war-heads stowed away beneath Langstrothdale Chase. Nuclear war-heads, which was nasty. Of course, Mrs Heffer had known about these but preferred not to talk about them and she had snubbed the vice-admiral all the way from King's Cross in case he mentioned them in her presence. Now, she looked around York station and uttered compliments. "Such a very *splendid* canopy, I always think. Such *luck* that the French never destroyed it."

"The French, ma'am?"

Mrs Heffer was pleased at the 'ma'am'. She explained, "I mean the Germans, of course. The *Luftwaffe*, Lord Mayor. And of course the Minster, such a *magnificent* building, don't you think?" She had done some research whilst on the train. "I always *so admire* the memorial to Sir Christopher Cradock . . . the vice-admiral at Coronel, don't you know. Such a very brave and gallant sailor. The Germans again, of course." Pleasantries over, Mrs Heffer processed out to the station forecourt where the limousine was drawn up. This had been provided by the military command at Catterick and was to be driven by a sergeant of the Royal Corps of Transport, a ramrod already in his seat and staring woodenly ahead as a lance-corporal leapt forward to open the door and salute. Mrs Heffer got in with the Home Secretary, the Defence Secretary and the Chief of the General Staff. Lesser cars behind awaited the lesser fry.

With its close police escort and the outriders, the motorcade swept away beneath the ancient walls of York, not a word having been spoken about explosives, threats and dangers. And Mrs Heffer turned her face away from a group of dirty-looking peace women gathered outside the station approach with banners reading TAKE YOUR WAR MATERIALS AWAY FROM OUR BEAUTIFUL DALES and another, less elegant, reading BULLOCKS TO MRS HEFFER.

FIFTEEN

Shard, as the coach went fast through West Witton heading for the market town of Hawes and the left fork for the region of Langstrothdale Chase and Cam Fell, was in a quandary. Hedge was incommunicado, up front as he was. Shard would have thought Hedge had done it on purpose in order to avoid having to make an irrevocable decision had he not seen Reverend Father virtually pinning his cousin next to him.

But what to do now?

Go ahead without Hedge? He wouldn't have been much use in any case but on the other hand any assistance was better than none. Now all he had was Brother Peter, alongside him with his gun in an aisle seat about half way along the coach. And Brother Peter could cop out at the last moment, losing his courage when the final moment loomed. Brother Peter was not a very brave man. As the coach proceeded, Shard and Brother Peter sat in silence; they couldn't talk about plans with the monks close around them. Brother Peter, Shard noted, was shaking like a leaf, not a very propitious sign. In the end, however, it was Brother Peter who gave Shard his opportunity. Brother Peter, with West Witton, Aysgarth and Bainbridge behind them, began wriggling about in his seat.

"What's the matter?" Shard asked.

"Want to wee-wee, don't I. There's a loo in Hawes."

"Know it, do you?"

"I'll say I do. Nearly got done there once."

"Done?"

"One of those nasty old men."

Tongue in cheek Shard said, "I'd have thought that an opportunity not to be missed."

"Oooh, you wouldn't say that if you'd seen the man." Brother Peter giggled and went on squirming. He tapped the shoulder of the brother next ahead, who happened to be Brother Infirmarer. He explained his need.

"You an' your bladder," Brother Infirmarer said witheringly. But he passed the message on. It went from mouth to mouth. "Brother Peter wants a slash, there's a pisser in Hawes." It reached Brother Werribee, sitting in the off-side front seat across the aisle from Reverend Father and Hedge.

"Little poufter."

This was loudly said. Brother Peter heard it and yelled back defiance. "I'm bloody *bursting* and it's bad for me and it's not fair, is it, Reverend Father?"

Reverend Father turned in his seat. "Let him go if he has to, Brother Werribee, he'll only wet his pants."

"Oooh, thank God for that," Brother Peter said, still squirming. He wriggled his way into Hawes. It was early yet but there was another coach parked near the public lavatory, a splendid one with KING OF THE ROAD on its side, from Worthing in West Sussex. Lines of old age pensioners waited, one a queue of ladies, the other of gents. Shard assessed the situation carefully as the coach began its approach to relief. Brother Peter, now that the halt had been authorised, was not the only one who wished to take advantage. Hedge was one, Brother Chamberlain another. Shard indicated that he wished to join. In his case permission was not unnaturally refused. Shard watched from the window while Brother Peter, who had handed over his gun to Brother Infirmarer, joined the queue of OAPs. If Brother Peter had any gumption at all, he would vanish and contact the police, by telephone if there wasn't an actual policeman around. It would not be a very difficult task and wouldn't require much brain. Brother Peter chatted amiably with two old men at the end of the gents' queue. Behind him stood Brother Chamberlain and Hedge. The driver of the King of the Road coach

169

wandered along for a cheery word with the monastery party's driver.

"Wotcher, mate. What you got in there, eh?"

"Bank clerks' outing." No more social workers; there had been a slight hiatus in the Fountains Abbey car park, the custodian querying the fact that the driver had been bringing out an empty coach. The driver had explained that the social workers had wanted to exercise their legs after sitting on their arses in their offices for a year and they had decided to walk down to the other gate, a fairly distant one, past the ruins themselves, at Studley Royal. This had in fact been accepted without comment or indeed much real interest but just to be on the safe side, the social workers were out. The drivers chatted; the monastery driver, a Brother Samuelson, had once been in Worthing on holiday, with his lady friend he said, and he knew all about Old Age Pensioners. "Couldn't move for the buggers," he said. "Like bleeding ants they was. Ants with zimmer frames."

"We all come to it," the Worthing driver said.

"Sure. But for me, not Worthing. Too much competition."

Brother Peter neared the gents and then vanished behind the wall of the public lavatory. Behind him went Brother Chamberlain. Shard's heart sank: Brother Chamberlain was sticking too close to Brother Peter for the latter to have much hope of a getaway. After an interval, Brother Chamberlain and Hedge were seen leaving the gents without Brother Peter. They approached the coach and climbed up. Brother Chamberlain reported to Reverend Father.

"Wanted a crap an' all, Reverend Father."

"Go and hurry him up," Reverend Father said, and Shard's hopes took another dive.

Mrs Heffer's motorcade left York on the A59 to Green Hammerton and Harrogate, where it turned right to continue on to Skipton. Here it took the A65 for Giggleswick, travelling very fast until, at Giggleswick, it turned on to the B6479 for Horton-in-Ribblesdale and the marquee now in place near the Ribblehead viaduct. "It's a very long way, Rufus," Mrs Heffer remarked for the tenth time to the Home

170